THE SECRET OF CHESTNUT LODGE

"How come we all sleep downstairs, Mr. Kinkaid?" Danny asked. "Does your Aunt Polly have other people staying at Chestnut Lodge?"

Reuben laughed. "Other people? Chestnut Lodge has been closed for twenty years. Aunt Polly had all she could do to get just this one floor in shape for guests."

"Twenty years!" Chris gasped. "Did it have a curse on it or something?"

Reuben Kinkaid didn't laugh. He didn't even smile. "Not exactly, Chris, but maybe it would be better not to say anything like that to Aunt Polly . . ."

THE PARTRIDGE FAMILY #14

THIRTEEN AT KILLER GORGE

by Vic Crume

CURTIS BOOKS
NEW YORK, N.Y.

CAST OF CHARACTERS

THE PARTRIDGES—

Shirley Partridge—Is "Mom" to five talented children. When the Partridge Family is on tour, it's Shirley who's behind the wheel of the big bus painted in psychedelic colors. Her bright, strong singing voice has helped make the Partridge Family famous from coast to coast.

Keith Partridge—Shirley's oldest son is "man of the family." A great help to his widowed mother, Keith plays guitar for the group.

Laurie Partridge—Shirley is proud of her pretty teenage daughter. Laurie's singing is an important part of the Partridge fame.

Danny Partridge—Like his older brother, Danny is great on guitar, and at ten years old, he has a steel-trap mind for business.

Christopher Partridge—Is an eight-year-old winner on the drums. He keeps the beat for the group.

Tracy Partridge—Baby of the family, she gives the group plenty of singing support wherever the Partridge Family performs.

Shirley Partridge recorded a song in the family garage with her five talented children—and the family was destined for stardom from the first scratch of a needle! Now they travel in a renovated old school bus painted in bright psychedelic colors. Shirley drives them all over the country in search of life, liberty, and the pursuit of singing engagements.

Chapter 1

Miss Polly Kinkaid twitched a hickory rocking chair closer to the porch railing. "Reuben," she called cheerfully to her nephew. "Didn't you ever hear that a watched pot never boils? Come sit down. The Partridge family won't get here a bit sooner for your marching up and down like a caged lion."

Reuben Kinkaid laughed and turned toward his elderly aunt. "*Me* a caged lion?" He pulled up another rocker. "Thanks for not calling me a nervous hen, Aunt Polly."

She patted her starchy pink dress. "Well, I must say, that would have fit, too. And why you're worrying so, I can't imagine. From all you've said, Mrs. Partridge must be a good driver, and I've always heard bus drivers have an excellent safety record."

Reuben groaned. "Aunt Polly, Shirley Partridge is *not* a bus driver. She drives a bus. There's a difference."

Aunt Polly shook her head. "That may be, but I'm

just saying that any woman who is talented, beautiful, famous, and brings up five young ones single-handed and drives a bus—well, you don't need to worry about her. And let that be the last of this discussion because here they come."

Reuben stood up. "Where? I don't see them."

Aunt Polly pointed over toward the right. "I just caught a glimpse. They just rounded Hairpin Bend, and that means they'll be here in no time at all. I'd best run out to the kitchen and tell Mrs. Griggs she can put on the potatoes and begin stripping the corn anytime now."

Aunt Polly was right. In less than five minutes, the Partridge family came bouncing up the drive of Chestnut Lodge—but not in the famous Partridge Family Bus. Instead, Keith Partridge was at the wheel of a bright blue pick-up truck, and his mother, Shirley Partridge, was seated beside him. The other four members of the family, hair blowing in the wind, clutched the sides of the open back and rocked cheerfully in the midst of stacks of luggage and burlap padding. As they came up the drive, Laurie, Shirley's teenage daughter, Tracy, the baby of the family, and the two "middles," Danny and Christopher, sang out in one voice, "Hi! Mr. Kinkaid! Hi!"

"Hi, Reuben. Here at last!" Shirley called, waving out the window.

Keith brought the truck to a stop, and Reuben hurried down the wooden porch steps. "Where's the bus?" he asked.

Shirley burst out laughing. "'Where's the bus?' What a welcome!" She stepped down from the truck.

"Well—welcome," Reuben grinned. "Welcome to

Chestnut Lodge. Aunt Polly and I have been watching for you for the last two hours, and she's been expecting to see the Partridge Bus with you at the wheel. Where is it?"

"Safe in MacFarlane's Garage in that little town of Honeybee back down at the bottom of this mountain. And there it will stay until Mr. MacFarlane can get a new water pump ordered for it. In fact, as far as I'm concerned, that wild, psychedelic elephant will never be driven up *this* mountain road. Wow! What a climb."

"Mr. MacFarlane rented us this nice truck, Mr. Kinkaid," Tracy called down from the back of the pickup. "Will you help us down?"

"Jump, silly," Chris and Danny said together. "Like this—." Both boys swung lightly to the ground.

"See! It's easy," Danny said, looking back up at Tracy and Laurie.

Keith came to his two sisters' rescue. He swung Tracy to the ground, then turned back to Laurie. "Don't think you're going to get this service all the time, Miss Partridge," he grinned as Laurie planted her hands on his shoulders. "You weigh a ton."

"You're getting very delicate lately, Mr. Partridge," Laurie replied. "I've been noticing it all day. Especially this noon when you ordered a third hamburger. I said to myself, 'My brother is certainly fading away. I mustn't forget and step on him sometime accidentally.'"

"You talk a lot, too," Keith said good-naturedly. "Come on. Jump."

Laurie steadied herself, then in a flash swung to the drive. "Hi, Mr. Kinkaid," she held out her hand. "Say, you didn't tell us that Chestnut Lodge was just about on top of the world!" She waved a hand in a sweeping half-circle. "Just *look* at all those mountains."

Everybody, even Reuben Kinkaid, who was usually too busy with endless plans for the Partridge Family's musical career to even notice scenery, was silent for a moment. The setting sun fell upon fold upon fold of quiet smoky-blue mountains. And as the newcomers looked out over the valley below, one twinkling golden light sprang to life.

"Just like a honeybee!" Tracy exclaimed. "Now I know why Mr. MacFarlane's town is called 'Honeybee.' Isn't that *pretty*."

Danny groaned loudly. "I suppose you think they got the town all settled first, then rushed up the mountain to think up a name. It's probably because their main industry is honey or something. You have to think of *economics*, Tracy."

Reuben laughed. "Wait until my Aunt Polly meets you, Danny. I'll bet that in all of her eighty years she hasn't thought as much about money as you have in twelve."

"What's that about eighty years?" Aunt Polly suddenly appeared at the top of the porch steps. She turned to Shirley. "What's that boy been saying about me, Mrs. Partridge?" She smiled. "Well come on in, everybody. We're certainly glad to see you."

Chris giggled under his breath as he followed Reuben Kinkaid up the steps. " 'That boy!' " he whispered to Danny.

Reuben half-turned. "Chris, Danny, everybody, meet my Aunt Polly."

10

Aunt Polly beamed. "My goodness! I'm just going to shake hands one at a time and get names straight right here and now."

She greeted each Partridge, then nodded her head. "I've got it all under my bonnet—who's who. My! I'll bet there are some pretty big appetites here. Reuben will show you your rooms, then everybody scamper straight back to the dining room! Dinner's about on the table. Lead the way, Reuben!"

"Say . . . this is great, Mr. Kinkaid!" Danny exclaimed as he looked around the room he and Chris were to share. "Did you notice? Every bedroom we passed had a place to wash right *in* it."

"The main bathroom's down the hall," Reuben explained. "That's for Saturday nights," he grinned.

"You mean we only have to take a bath once a week here?" Chris asked, looking pleased.

"That's up to you-know-who," Reuben grinned.

"How come we all sleep downstairs, Mr. Kinkaid?" Danny asked. "Does your Aunt Polly have other people staying at Chestnut Lodge?"

Reuben laughed. "Other people? Chestnut Lodge has been closed for twenty years. Aunt Polly had all she could do to get just this one floor in shape for guests."

"Twenty years!" Chris gasped. "Did it have a curse on it or something?"

Reuben Kinkaid didn't laugh. He didn't even smile. "Not exactly, Chris," he said slowly. "But maybe it would be better not to say anything like that to Aunt Polly. I had a hard time coaxing her to come back to

Chestnut Lodge, and . . . well, anyhow, just don't ask her questions. I'll tell you all about it sometime. Now hurry up, kids. Dinner any minute."

As he strode off down the hall, Danny watched him from the doorway.

"What are you looking at?" Chris asked.

Danny closed the door and turned back into the room. "I wanted to see if he'd 'scamper' like his Aunt Polly said everybody should."

"Well, did he?" Chris asked.

"No, but he hurried."

"You know what I think, Dan?" Chris asked. "I think Mr. Kinkaid's Aunt Polly had a tragic romance or something. Maybe the man she was going to marry fell off this mountain, and she turned the key in the front door never to return again."

Danny shook his head. "Honest, Chris! You never put two and two together. Mr. Kinkaid said that his Aunt Polly was eighty years old. Then he said this place had been closed for twenty years."

Chris looked blank. "Well?"

"Well, twenty years ago, she would have been sixty. I don't think that ladies sixty years old go around having tragic romances." He shook his head. "No, there must be some other reason. Maybe the bottom fell out of the stock market, and his Aunt Polly went broke."

Chris turned on the water tap. It sputtered and spurted. "Danny, you're smart—even if you did just subtract twenty from eighty when you were telling me I should be adding two and two. But you're smarter about money and stuff like that than you are about people. Mr. Kinkaid looked pretty funny when he said it wasn't exactly a curse and said not to mention it." He splashed water on his face and groped for a towel. "Nope! I think something awful happened here. Maybe during the Civil War—this place looks old enough."

Danny groaned and flung himself on a bed. "Oh wow. The Civil War. That was a *hundred* years ago."

"Okay," Chris answered calmly. "So I don't know history either. But there's *something* funny about this place. I can feel it."

"All I feel is hungry," Danny grinned. "Are you through washing?"

Down the hall, Laurie perched herself in the window seat and watched her mother brush wind-snarls from Tracy's yellow hair. "Mom . . ." she hesitated. "Miss Polly is awfully nice. But . . ."

"But what, dear?" Shirley asked.

"But Chestnut Lodge just doesn't look like . . . well . . . much fun. I noticed . . . there isn't even a swimming pool. And . . . and I thought that at a lodge there'd be interesting people around."

"So?"

"So what's there to do for a whole *month*, Mom?"

Shirley smiled. "Reuben has never failed us yet, has he."

"*Failed us!*" Laurie exclaimed. "Mom, he's sent us to perfectly *too* strange places before this. You know he has."

"Well, I don't see anything strange about Chestnut Lodge, Laurie. And besides, he said he has a big surprise for us, and I'm anxious to hear what it is."

Laurie turned to the window and looked out at the

darkening line of the mountains in the distance. She sighed. "I'm afraid that the big surprise may be that he wants us to disappear from the world, or something. Just look! *Nothing* but mountains. Honestly, mother. It's all right for the kids and for you older people, but for Keith and me—it's like time out of our lives!"

Shirley patted her oldest daughter's shoulder. "Laurie, I promise. If it's too much time out of your lives, we won't stay. Meantime, would you mind sparing this one evening to the kids and the old folks? Okay?"

Laurie flushed. "You're laughing at me, Mom."

"Of course I'm not laughing at . . ." Shirley broke off, and her face lighted in the special, honest, happy smile her family privately called 'Mom's look.' "Well, honey, maybe I was. But don't worry. I have faith in Reuben's surprises, and I'm anxious to hear what this one is. Let's start for the dining room."

Of all the Partridges, Keith was the only one not thinking about the past or the future. He propped two guitar cases in one corner of the room, then heaved a heavy suitcase up to an old oak luggage bench. "This place is sure antiquated," he thought as he opened the clasps and took out a fresh shirt. "But I like it. It isn't dismal and it isn't spooky. And I like Reuben's Aunt Polly. She may be eighty but there's nothing tottery about her. She sort of taps along—I don't know—sort of frisky, like a kitten."

He walked over to the washbasin, turned the tap on, and looked at himself in the mirror. He shook his head and laughed. "A kitten!" he exclaimed aloud. "Partridge, you fall for all the girls!"

14

Chapter 2

☐ Reuben Kinkaid finished the last bite of peach shortcake. "That was wonderful, Aunt Polly," he said. "I'm beginning to think I should move to Chestnut Lodge permanently."

Aunt Polly laughed gaily. "And a fine time you'd have when the winter winds begin to blow. I'll be heading down the mountain long before that."

Reuben sighed. "There goes a whole new idea, I guess." He leaned back in his chair. "Well, folks, I told you I had a really big surprise for you, didn't I?"

Everybody nodded.

Reuben looked down at his coffee cup, and his face seemed to be turning a deep pink.

"Goodness gracious, Reuben," Aunt Polly chirped, "Are you planning to let the summer go by with us sitting here waiting for you to begin? Out with it!"

Reuben cleared his throat. "Well, this is going to be a surprise *to* everybody, but not *for* everybody," he said. "But I hope you'll all like it."

Shirley looked at him sharply. "Reuben Kinkaid, what have you been up to? I want to know this minute."

Reuben Kinkaid looked across at her. "Okay, Shirley. Can I count on you not to let me down?"

Shirley shook her head. "No," she said firmly. "Tell us first."

Reuben took a deep breath. "It's a movie," he said in a rush.

"A movie!" everybody chorused.

"You mean we're going to make a movie?" Keith asked, his emerald eyes sparkling.

Reuben flushed a deeper red. "Well, not exactly *everybody*," he said. "But there's a great part in it for your mother and for Laurie. And I even managed a bit part for Tracy."

There was a shocked silence around the table. Nobody smiled. Even little Tracy looked stern. "What happens to Keith and Danny and Christopher?" she asked. "Why can't they be in it?"

"Well, let me begin at the beginning," Reuben Kinkaid said. "Frameway Films is going to do one of the biggest pictures about ecology and nature and people, and stuff like that, right here in the Great Smokies. And there's a great part in it for you, Shirley. You'd be playing the part of the dead grandmother."

The silence around the table seemed to quiver. Then every single Partridge exploded into laughter. Shirley rocked back and forth, holding her sides. "I can't wait," she gasped. "My big break in pictures, and I'm a dead grandmother."

"Does Mom get any lines," Danny hooted, "Or does she just float around?"

"Very funny, Daniel," Reuben Kinkaid said. "Now if I may be allowed to be heard over this cackling . . ."

"It had better get better," Shirley giggled.

"It so happens that this is a very serious story about ecology, as I said. Laurie plays the part of a mountain girl who . . ."

"Plays the dulcimer," Keith chuckled.

Reuben looked surprised. "How did you know?" he asked.

"All mountain girls play the dulcimer. I've seen them on the Late, Late Show."

"What's a dulcimer?" Chris asked.

Reuben didn't explain. He turned to Laurie. "When a lumber company sends a surveying party up the mountain, you help the head surveyor—you show him your favorite waterfalls and trees and stuff like that, not knowing his company is going to wreck the whole place. But the more he sees the beauty of the land, the more he hates the idea. Actually—I won't go into detail—you save thousands of acres of untouched wilderness by teaching him the real values of life."

"Who teaches the lumber company?" Danny asked.

"The same guy," Reuben answered. "He just happens to be the son of the owner."

"Oh, wow. Who plays him?" Laurie asked.

"Courtney Cross," Reuben replied.

"*Courtney Cross!*" Laurie gasped. "Oh, he's marvelous."

"There goes Laurie," Danny sighed.

"I haven't gone anywhere!" Laurie exclaimed angrily. "Anyhow, Mr. Kinkaid, even if there were parts for all of us, I couldn't take that one. I don't

17

even know what a dulcimer is, let alone how to play one."

"No problem there, Laurie. I have someone all lined up to teach you and your mother too. You see, in the movie there's supposed to have been a mountain feud years before, and . . . well, anyhow, that's where the grandmother's part comes in." He turned to Shirley. "And in those scenes, Tracy would play the part of Laurie's mother as a child."

"Would I get to tell Laurie it's her bedtime?" Tracy asked with great interest.

Danny and Chris doubled over in fits of giggles. Keith bellowed mirthfully, and Laurie and Shirley leaned into each other, laughing.

"Well, what do you say?" Reuben asked, raising his voice. "None of the parts are really big, of course, so it isn't as though this would interfere with your Labor Day rock concert. How about it?"

Shirley sat up straight in her chair, and her laughter vanished. "Reuben, I know you've gone to a lot of trouble to do this for us. But you should have *asked*. I just don't like the idea of our going in separate directions. After all, we're the Partridge *Family*."

Miss Polly, who hadn't said a word since Reuben complimented the peach shortcake, suddenly spoke up. "Reuben," she said sharply, "Where is this wonderful movie about the Great Smokies to be made?"

To everybody's surprise, Reuben Kinkaid's face turned a fiery red. He looked down at his coffee cup again, then in a slow voice he said, "That's one of the very important things, Aunt Polly. They want to film Big Gorge. That's how I got onto the whole thing. As your business agent, I was the one they got in touch

18

with when they found that Big Gorge was on your land. They're going to pay you a tidy sum for the use of it, and I have everything all fixed up."

Miss Polly sat up stiffly in her chair. "Then you'll have to un-fix it," she said sternly. "You know well enough how I feel about the gorge. I'll not have movie people nor anybody else traipsing around there. No permission of mine has been given. Furthermore, Reuben Kinkaid, when you coaxed me to open Chestnut Lodge after so many years, you said that you wanted a place where you could invite the Partridges to visit. Not a word else was said, and now it's plain to be seen that the Partridges don't like your scheme a bit more than I do."

Reuben Kinkaid pushed back his chair. "Okay. I give up. Ruin me! Because that's what you're all doing, you know. Nobody will ever take my word again as business manager for the Partridge Family, nor as business manager for you, Aunt Polly." He stood up and strode to the window. "And what do all of you care about bringing a little prosperity to Honeybee? Forget it! I'm only sorry I've caused so much trouble. I'll cancel the plans, Aunt Polly, even though it would mean you'd have a chance to make enough money to set up a college scholarship for Honeybee kids—maybe make the gorge pay back for . . . Let's forget it."

"Wait a minute!" Keith Partridge exclaimed. "Mom, I don't see that Reuben is breaking up the family. As he said, you and Laurie would be through here before our Labor Day concert."

"And I would be too," Tracy added helpfully. "I wouldn't break up the act."

19

Shirley burst out laughing and Aunt Polly smiled faintly.

"Of course, Miss Polly," Keith said, "If you don't want to rent your property, that's something else again. But I'd like to see Mom and my sisters get a break in pictures. And I'll bet Reuben has worked hard to manage this."

"I'll bet he has too!" Danny exclaimed. "And it isn't as though we wouldn't be a family. You can't stop being a family just because your mother's in a movie."

"And your sisters," Chris added.

Aunt Polly hesitated. She looked at Shirley. "How about it, Mrs. Partridge? Do you want to learn to play the dulcimer?"

Shirley dimpled. "Do you want to rent your land?"

Aunt Polly shook her head. "No, I don't. But I will. There's just one thing, Reuben. I'll have no responsibility about movie folks or anybody else traipsing around the gorge." She turned to Shirley. "And that means anybody. You see to it that your little girl keeps close by, Mrs. Partridge. That gorge is a killer."

"For goodness sake, Aunt Polly!" Reuben exclaimed impatiently. "Do you think a movie company would let any actor be in one second's danger?"

"Of course," Aunt Polly answered calmly. "Stunt men. I've read about it."

"Well, Tracy is no stunt man. Don't worry."

"When do the movie people get here, Mr. Kinkaid?" Danny asked.

"Probably late next week," Reuben answered, glad to get off on another subject. "That will give your mother and sister time to . . ."

"Learn to play the dulcimer," the family chorused.

20

Reuben grinned. It would take more than a movie to break up the Partridge Family!

But snuggled under woolly blankets in the chill mountain night, Shirley Partridge couldn't get Miss Polly's words out of her thoughts. A killer gorge!

"Mama," Tracy whispered. "Are you asleep?"

Shirley opened her eyes and saw the small moonlit figure of her daughter standing beside her bed. "No, honey. And why aren't you?"

"What's a killer gorge, Mama?" Tracy whispered.

Shirley flung back the covers. "Jump in," she invited.

Tracy cuddled close to her. "Honey, you wouldn't mind if Mama told Mr. Kinkaid it was too early for you to start a movie career, would you?" Shirley asked.

"You mean because of the killer gorge?" Tracy asked worriedly. "But what about you, Mama?"

Shirley laughed. "You couldn't get me anywhere near any old gorge. Don't you worry about *me*."

"Promise?" Tracy asked sleepily.

"Promise," Shirley replied.

And in no time at all, the oldest and youngest members of the Patridge family were sound asleep.

Down the hall, Danny and Chris knocked on Keith's door.

"Why aren't you guys asleep?" Keith asked, opening the door and looking down at his pajama-clad brothers.

"We just thought we'd ask you if you had any ideas," Danny said.

"About what?" Keith asked yawning.

"About what to do while Mom and the girls are making the movie," Chris said.

"Can't we decide tomorrow?"

"Sure," Danny replied. "But I have a great idea, and I figured you might be interested. You see, this state is absolutely full of jewelry—I mean the stuff they make jewelry out of. There are all kinds of semi-precious stones. I've read about it. So I was thinking—we could go into business. We might as well make some money while we're here. And Chris and I have picked out a name for us. We could call the business the Partridge Family Rocks. We'd hunt rocks and with a name like that, I'll bet we could sell everything we could dig up."

Keith shook his head. "I don't think they come out of the ground ready-to-wear."

"They don't!" Chris exclaimed in a shocked voice.

"Of course they don't," Danny said impatiently. "But we can easily arrange to get them shined up, probably at a very small investment. How about it, Keith? Are you interested?"

"In investing?" Keith grinned. "Let's talk about it tomorrow. We might find a lot of things we'd want to do around here."

Danny shook his head. "I hope you're right, but it doesn't look too hopeful to me."

Long after her visitors were asleep, Miss Polly Kinkaid lay awake. "That Reuben," she sighed. "He can just charm this old bird off the bough. First he coaxes me up here, then he gets me to say 'yes' to a *movie* made right on my land. He knew very well how the idea of a college scholarship for Honeybee children would appeal to me."

She suddenly sat up in bed. "Now if that isn't ridiculous! I never asked him what they'd be paying me."

She leaned back against the pillows and frowned. "But I'll have nothing to do with anything anywhere near the gorge. I'll never look on it again as long as I live. Never! *Not with all those ghosts down there.*"

And in the night silence it seemed to Miss Polly that she could faintly hear the far away, surging roar of Big Gorge. From high overhead came the sound of a heavy, dull thud. "Goodness!" Miss Polly thought sleepily. "How these old timbers do expand and contract. Maybe I should have Reuben check the attic beams one of these days."

She closed her eyes.

Chapter 3

☐ Miss Polly had nearly finished her breakfast by the time her great-nephew came out to the sunny back porch beyond the dining room.

"Say, it's cool enough out here for a sweater!" Reuben exclaimed.

Miss Polly nodded. "Better go get one. And pick up your breakfast tray in the kitchen, Reuben. No table service at Chestnut Lodge for breakfast or lunch. I told Mrs. Partridge last night."

She reached over to the small radio that was set in the dining room window sill. "I'll just get the morning news while you're getting your breakfast."

The Partridges and Reuben came out on the porch at the same time. Aunt Polly snapped off the radio.

"Another skyjacking," she said, shaking her head. "And this one somewhere right here in these mountains. They say he hopped out with one parachute and three-hundred thousand dollars."

Danny gasped. "Right here!" he exclaimed.

Miss Polly waved her arm in a sweeping half-circle. "Right *there*, maybe."

Chris's eyes widened as he looked over the tremendous view of mountains. "Man, nobody would ever find him, would they?"

Danny shook his head. "Looks more to me like *he'd* never find anybody. Miss Polly, I guess there's just about no population around here, is there?"

Miss Polly laughed. "There are plenty of people, and plenty of towns and settlements too. You just don't see them from here." Then she looked very serious. "But more than likely he might not find one of them—not if he came down in the rhododendron thickets. In the old days, they earned the name 'Rhododendron hells.' Just like a jungle they are, and I'd be inclined to pity even a skyjacker caught in them."

"Pity?" Reuben repeated. "How much pity does a skyjacker have? I pity the passengers and the crews."

Shirley glanced at Danny who was staring thoughtfully at the mountains. "If you're thinking of finding the airline's money, forget it." She turned to Miss Polly. "Now that it looks as though I'm going to be working, I'm wondering about the boys, Miss Polly. I don't want them to be a bother to you, but I'd appreciate your advice to them on where and where not to go."

Miss Polly nodded. "There are plenty of trails, and there's no need to get lost." She looked at the boys. "There are plenty of snakes too. So you keep to the trails, and let the snakes enjoy themselves elsewhere. Wouldn't hurt to carry a stout stick."

Shirley nearly choked on her coffee. "Miss Polly!" she gasped. "This all sounds dangerous to me. Wouldn't it be better if they just played in the yard?"

"In the *yard!*" Danny exclaimed. "Mom! Just how young do you think we are?"

Luckily for the boys, Keith appeared at that moment. "Mom, did I just hear you say I'm supposed to play in the yard?" He grinned broadly.

"Well . . ."

"Don't worry. Dan and Chris and I have plans." He turned to Miss Polly. "Is there a library in Honeybee?"

Danny and Chris exchanged alarmed glances. Was Keith planning for them to spend their mountain vacation in the Children's Reading Room?

"There's a nice little library," Miss Polly replied. "It's right in the south corner of the Courthouse. I stopped in there last week, but I declare, I can't remember which day it was, and it isn't open every day. You can telephone the County Clerk's Office. They'll know. And as long as you're going down to Honeybee, you might inquire of Mr. MacFarlane about riding horses, if you like riding. His brother keeps saddle horses. And then when you come back I'll show you a mighty fine swimming hole, that is, if you like to swim."

"Man!" Chris exclaimed. "Things *are* looking up."

"Speaking of 'up'," Reuben Kinkaid said, "I hope you and Laurie brought along good walking shoes, Shirley. We'll drive to the Jennings' cabin, but it's about a half-block walk up the mountain from the road."

Miss Polly chuckled. "A half-block walk! I'd like to see the Jennings' faces when they hear such city-talk from you."

"What's the Jennings' cabin?" Danny asked.

"Where the Jennings live," his mother answered. "And it's where Jenny Jennings is going to teach your sister and mother how to play the dulcimer."

"I'd be interested sometime, too," Keith said. "At least, I'd be interested in hearing real mountain music. When are you going?"

"Soon as Laurie has her breakfast," Reuben Kinkaid replied. "Any chance, Shirley, of her being up before noon?"

"Oh, wow. What some people won't say about other people. Hi, everybody." Laurie came out to the porch carrying her tray.

"If you'll tell me where the phone is, I'll find out about library hours, Miss Polly," Keith said.

"Help yourself. Right behind the desk counter in the lobby."

It was the signal for activity. The boys tagged after Keith, Shirley and Reuben left the table urging Laurie not to dawdle, and Miss Polly went to the kitchen to supervise the packing of a peach pie for Mrs. Jennings, her mountain neighbor.

No sooner had Reuben and the "dulcimer students" left along with Tracy, than Keith and the boys emerged on the porch ready to go exploring.

"The library isn't open until tomorrow," Danny explained. "We thought we'd just look around here."

Miss Polly looked up from the big sack of peas she

was shelling into an aluminum pan. She eyed them shrewdly. "And so I suppose wild horses couldn't keep you from looking for the gorge, could they?"

Keith looked uncomfortable. "Oh, we just thought we'd look things over, Miss Polly."

Miss Polly ran a pink thumb along a pea pod. Peas rattled into the pan like an elfin burst of gunfire. "Well, I'm going to tell you where it is, and I'm going to extract a promise from you. Agreed?" Her bright blue eyes looked straight into Keith's, then Danny's, then Chris's.

The boys nodded. "Say it," Miss Polly commanded.

"Agreed," they answered.

Miss Polly lifted a small, thin hand. She pointed to the left. "See that path?"

They nodded.

"You follow it straight along apiece, then when you're out of sight of this old place and out of *my* sight, you'll come to a fork in the path. One fork climbs up and one goes down. Should you take the down path you come out almost on the level with the gorge. *Don't take that path.* Instead, you climb the high trail. It's a sight longer, and it brings you up high above the gorge and ends in a lookout place. But you can see the whole boil from there."

Without another word, Miss Polly set down the bowl of peas and marched into the Lodge.

The boys looked at each other. "Man, Miss Polly sure knows how to say what she means," Danny said in a low voice.

Chris gulped. "I got the feeling she'd see us if we took the wrong path."

29

Keith started down the steps. "Miss Polly's depending on our keeping our word—not on her magic powers. Come on."

It wasn't a long hike even going the long way, but the climb past the fork was steep and hard-going. Before the boys reached the top, they began to hear a dull, heavy roar in the distance.

"We must be getting close," Danny puffed.

Almost as he spoke, the shadowy trail suddenly rose out of the dark greenery and ended in an open, blowy world of blue sky, and far below the stone-walled lookout platform, Big Gorge tumbled and raged between rock walls.

"Man!" the three boys exclaimed in one voice.

Eighty feet below, white water leaped and boiled furiously. Over to the left they could see a stretch of swift moving dark water. Then suddenly it burst into white plumes of spray, ran smoothly on again, then plunging downward over boulders, fell into a sickening, swirling giant eddy before smoothing out once again, and flowed off out of sight around a curve in the rock wall.

"And Mom and the girls are going to be down there?" Chris asked, his voice low.

Keith shook his head. " 'Killer gorge' is right. I think everybody ought to think twice—including Frameway Films. I'm going to tell Mom to take a walk up here before she . . ."

"Look!" Danny shouted. He pointed toward the smooth water heading into the gorge.

Keith and Chris followed his pointing hand. Rushing along on the swift current was a giant, white bubble.

"It's a parachute!" Danny shouted. "It's the skyjacker!—Oh, *no!*"

It was no time to think about skyjacking as a cruel, criminal act. To the three watching boys, a paralyzing, unbelievable sight was unfolding—a fellow human was being rushed to his death before their eyes.

In seconds, they saw the chute catch in the boil, hang up for a scant moment on the rocks, then plunge straight into the glassy-sided circling current of the eddy. In horrible circling sweeps, it plunged lower and lower. Then suddenly, like a last soap bubble sucked down a drain, the parachute, and whatever ghastly cargo it carried, disappeared.

The boys stared in horror. Sky, rocks, water, trees —everything was exactly as it had been before. It was as though the dreadful thing they had seen had never happened.

There was an awful silence. Then Keith turned away. Danny and Chris followed. Not a word was said as they scrunched back down the steep trail. When they reached the fork, Keith spoke. "We'll have to call the state police," he said. "Miss Polly is going to hate this, I guess."

Danny nodded. "Yes. She doesn't like people 'traipsing'—and I'll bet there'll be a lot of that now."

"The police will want to know exactly what we saw," Keith said.

Chris shivered. "We all know what we saw—we saw a guy get drowned."

Keith stopped walking. He turned around and looked at Chris. "Is that what you saw?"

Chris nodded. "Sure."

"How about you Danny?"

31

Danny nodded. "What else?"

Keith hesitated. "Well, I didn't."

His brother stared at him. "You *didn't?*"

Keith shook his head. "I just saw a parachute."

"Sure, that's all we *saw*," Danny said. "But we had to know somebody was being dragged along with it."

Keith shrugged. "Maybe so. But we didn't see anyone. We tell the police *what* we saw—and that's *all* we tell."

"I don't feel so good," Chris said.

"Aw, for gosh sakes, Chris," Danny blurted. "Who does?"

Then, single-file, the three continued along the steep trail to Chestnut Lodge and Miss Polly's telephone.

When Reuben, Shirley, Tracy, and Laurie came driving up, they saw Aunt Polly and the three boys lined up in rockers along the porch railing and looking for all the world like a string of sparrows on a telephone wire.

"What on earth!" Shirley exclaimed. "Miss Polly must have strange powers! I've never seen the boys *all* doing nothing at one time."

"They probably ate so much lunch they can't move," Laurie said cheerfully. "I wish you'd said 'yes' when Mrs. Jennings asked us to stay and eat. I'm starved."

"Hey, look who's coming up the Honeybee road," Reuben Kinkaid said as he cut off the motor.

Shirley and Laurie twisted around to look. "Why, it's a police car!" Shirley exclaimed. "My goodness! I hope nothing's wrong." She hurriedly stepped from the car and ran up the steps. "Hi, Miss Polly . . . boys."

"Hi," the boys answered flatly, not taking their eyes from the police cruiser with its revolving red roof light. It slowed to a stop behind Reuben's car, and two officers stepped out.

"What's wrong here?" Shirley asked anxiously.

Aunt Polly glanced up. "No need to worry, Mrs. Partridge. Just you sit down. We'll all hear what the boys have to tell the officers. It's been once-told already. Nobody's done anything wrong."

Officers Clingley and Smith stood up. "Well, that's a good, clear report, boys," Officer Clingley said. He snapped shut his notebook. "Miss Polly, we'll make a routine search below the gorge, and I guess everybody around here knows what will come of that. But you might have a little bother with searchers. After all, there're a lot of folks mighty interested in finding three-hundred thousand dollars—the airlines folks, and local people looking for a reward. And maybe there'll be newspaper people. But they needn't bother you, Miss Polly."

"Thank you, Lyle," Miss Polly said in a shaky voice. "Now, remember me to your grandmother when you see her. And it was nice to meet you, Officer Smith. Have you been living in this part of the state long?"

"No, ma'am," Officer Smith answered. "But I've heard about Big Gorge ever since I was a kid. That sure must have been . . ."

Officer Clingley seized his partner's arm. "Well, got to be going," he boomed. "Thank you, boys. Nice to have met all you folks. Wait 'til I tell my kids I met The Partridge Family!"

After a lunch of hamburgers, more hamburgers, wild strawberries and cream, Miss Polly announced she was ready for a nap.

"I wouldn't be a bit surprised if I didn't feel like walking over to the swimming hole around about two o'clock or so. Those who wish to go, have on your swimming costumes."

Without further words she went tapping off to her room.

Tracy looked worried. "Mama, we just brought our suits. I never thought we'd need costumes, did you?"

"Ssh, it's just another way of saying swimming suits," Shirley quickly explained.

The Partridges had never seen such a pretty place to swim. Aunt Polly's "swimming hole" turned out to be two broad, quiet pools, almost like two landings along a staircase. The upper pool was about three feet deep, and frilling along its upper edge was a tiny foot-high waterfall. Its waters spilled over into the second and deeper pool. A second small waterfall fed a shallow-running mountain stream.

Aunt Polly sat on the bank and watched her company splash around. "Miss Polly," Tracy called, scrambling up the banks and flinging waterdrops far and wide. "Do you know Maribelle Jennings? She's awfully nice and she's just my age. Can she come down and swim in your pool?"

"I don't know why not," Miss Polly said. "She's

welcome anytime. How did the dulcimer lesson go?"

"Oh fine," Tracy answered. "And just wait until Keith sees Jenny Jennings. Oh, wow, he'll be crazy about Jenny, she's so pretty."

"Maybe he'll take her to the square dance down in Honeybee Saturday night. The Jennings are having dinner with us tomorrow so he'll have a chance to ask her."

"Oh I bet he will," Tracy sighed. "I wish there was someone to ask Laurie, too."

Miss Polly smiled down at the little girl. Then she looked out over the splashing swimmers. "I just wish Reuben never had brought this nice family here," she thought. "That terrible gorge. Maybe there *is* some awful curse on that place."

And Miss Polly's pink face saddened.

Chapter 4

□ It was late afternoon when the swimmers walked up the side path and around to the front verandah of Chestnut Lodge. To everyone's surprise, a stranger arose from a rocker as they approached the steps. Laurie could see in one quick glance that he was much younger than Mr. Kinkaid, older than Keith, and *very* good-looking.

"Miss Kinkaid?" he asked politely.

Miss Polly nodded.

"I was told I might wait here for you. The person I talked with said she couldn't rent a room to me, but that I might wait and ask you."

Miss Polly shook her head. "I'm afraid you've waited in vain, sir. Chestnut Lodge is no longer open to the public. I'm sorry."

The stranger's face fell. "That's bad news for me. I was riding my bicycle along that road," he waved toward the Honeybee road, "And when I got to that steep, sharp turn . . ."

"Hairpin Bend," Laurie said, fluttering her lashes.

He nodded toward her and smiled. "I began walking the bike along—the road's so steep there. And what happens? A copperhead snake comes crawling out at me. Anyhow, I threw my bike at it, and . . . well, I don't have a bike anymore. It slid right under that cable fencing and took off into space—my backpack with it."

Miss Polly looked shocked. "A foolish loss, I must say, for I doubt a copperhead crawled *at* you, although he might happened to have been going in that direction. And if your bicycle didn't catch in a tree, it went down a long, long way."

The young man sighed. "I've already given it up as lost." He started for the steps. "Well, I'd better head back, I guess. Thanks for the nice rest I had on your porch."

Miss Polly hesitated. "It won't be too long before our evening meal. I'll be happy to have another place set, then perhaps my nephew would drive you down to Honeybee in the evening. You'll be sure to find a room there."

Laurie's face fell. She'd hoped Aunt Polly was going to change her mind and let the stranger stay, at least long enough to invite her to the square dance on Saturday. Slowly, she walked up the steps.

By the time Miss Polly and her guests were seated at the dinner table, everybody knew the latest arrival was a writer and that his real name was Tom Sadd.

"But I use the name T. G. Saddler in my writing," Tom said. "I write mostly articles on vacation fun places, and 'Sadd' isn't such a fun name," he laughed.

As for Tom Sadd, he heard about the movie that was to be made, the dulcimer lessons, and the terrible event in the gorge.

He shook his head. "Something has to be done to stop those air bandits. Was anybody on the plane hurt?"

Reuben Kinkaid shook his head. "No—luckily. No one but the skyjacker, and his troubles are over."

"I've been out of touch with news," Tom said. "Actually, I haven't heard what's been going on in the world since I pedaled my bike out of Ashville, and that was three days ago."

"Can we turn on the radio, Miss Polly?" Danny asked. It's almost newstime."

They didn't have long to wait for the news, and it was reported in detail. All three Partridge boys were mentioned, and a full account was given of their story.

"The skyjacker," the announcer said, "has now been identified as Ernest Tell of Buffalo, New York. Tell was described by his neighbors as a quiet, loner type."

The next voice was that of a neighbor. "Nobody really knew him. He minded his own business. Seemed nice enough. But that extra crazy hair and beard—he looked like he was wearing shrubbery on top of his shoulders."

The announcer's voice followed. "We have learned that the gorge in which the skyjacker was probably sucked down is well known in that area as a deadly stretch of water . . . Now to the political scene . . ."

Danny snapped the dial.

Tom Sadd shook his head. "You'll probably have people barging around here looking for the money, although it probably went down with him."

Laurie shuddered. "Can't we get on another subject?" she asked.

"Maybe moving out to the porch would help," Miss Polly suggested.

Danny and Chris sat down on the front steps as the others arranged the hickory rockers to suit themselves. "You said you wrote about fun places, Tom," Danny said. "Where were you headed for a fun place? The Honeybee road doesn't go on over the mountain, does it, Miss Polly?"

"Oh, I was researching for a different kind of article," Tom replied quickly. "This time it was to be on rock hunting." He sighed. "Of course, I can still do it, but I lost the collection I'd gathered so far when I lost the bike."

Danny and Chris exchanged quick glances. "What kinds did you expect to find around here?" Danny asked. "We're pretty interested in rock hunting ourselves."

"In fact, we're going into the business," Chris added.

Tom looked thoughtful. "I wish I could give you some help in getting started. There are plenty of interesting specimens in this area—aquamarines, garnets, rubies, sapphires."

Danny's eyes rounded. "You mean you can just pick them up if you keep your eyes open?"

Tom laughed. "Well, it's not quite that easy, no. They're not rolling around loose, or anything. That's another thing I lost—my tools and—*oh man!*" He jumped to his feet.

"What's wrong?" Reuben Kinkaid asked for everybody.

"My jacket," Tom Sadd groaned. "It was strapped over the backpack on the carrier." He hastily reached in a hip pocket and pulled out a folded black checkbook. "Well," he sighed, "I still have my traveler's checks." He shook his head. "But my wallet was in my jacket. This is awful. Man! My driver's license, my Social Security card, my . . . well, everything." He looked stunned. "Maybe I'd better try hiking down in the valley below Hairpin Bend."

"Tough luck," Reuben Kinkaid said. "But I can tell you the only way to get your stuff back is going by helicopter. Isn't it, Aunt Polly?"

"Not at all," Miss Polly replied. "Mr. Sadd could go down to Honeybee, work his way along the valley, then begin climbing *up*. 'Twould doubtless take all summer, though."

Tom sighed. "It would be quicker to write letters. After all, everything more or less is replaceable."

Miss Polly hesitated. "Well, I can't invite you to stay all summer, but I might reconsider your stopping for the night. Things always look more hopeful in the morning, don't you think?"

Things certainly did look more hopeful in the morning, and it all started with Miss Polly's talk with Reuben Kinkaid before the others had come in for breakfast.

"What with people wandering around the gorge looking for traces of that skyjacker and hoping to find money, and movie people arriving next week, I feel *very* unsettled, Reuben," she began. "Now Mr. Sadd

seems a nice enough young man, and I was thinking
. . . maybe we could offer him a job in exchange for
room and board and a small salary. That would give
him a chance to get himself organized. I mean to say,
he could spend his traveler's checks on a change of
clothing, for instance. And he'd be a great help with
Chris and Danny, because I'm afraid that when Keith
meets Jenny Jennings, he'll be taking dulcimer lessons
himself." Her blue eyes suddenly twinkled. "And besides, who'll take Laurie to the square dance tomorrow
night if Mr. Sadd leaves?"

Reuben Kinkaid looked thoughtful. "Well, I agree
that he seems a nice enough fellow. But, maybe he
wouldn't be interested, Aunt Polly. He may have his
own plans."

"I'll ask. That's the only way to find out," Miss
Polly said briskly.

By ones and twos, the Chestnut Lodge guests arrived for breakfast. "Mercy!" Miss Polly exclaimed.
"Here it is, eight o'clock, and here I sit! I do believe
I'll leave you folks and get to work. Mr. Sadd, could I
have a word with you when you've finished breakfast? I'll be on the porch."

Mid-morning, Chris came out on the porch. "Now
we have Tom, we don't need to go to the library," he
told Miss Polly. "We decided not to start rock hunting
right away, though. We're going swimming instead."

No sooner had the boys left, than Reuben, Shirley,
Laurie and Tracy started off to the Jennings' cabin.

"Wait until Keith meets Jenny tonight," Laurie giggled. "Oh wow."

"Why 'oh wow'?" Shirley asked.

42

"Nobody's told him that Jenny's a freshman in college, or will be, this fall. Keith probably thinks she spends all her time prancing barefoot over the mountains when she isn't a-feudin' and a-fightin' like in the late, late shows."

Shirley laughed. "Seems to me that the latest, latest show is about the same kind of idea except for the ecology angle. But you know, I was a little disappointed myself when I learned the Jennings were summer people and not real mountaineers."

"Oh they're real enough, all right," Reuben Kinkaid said. "Jenny's grandma and my Aunt Polly were girls together. The Jennings cabin has stood up there since before Chestnut Lodge was built. And Jenny probably knows as much about ecology around here as a visiting scientist would."

Laurie was struck by a sudden idea. "Couldn't you get some kind of job for Jenny with the movie people? Maybe she could advise them or something, and it would be a lot of fun if she were working with us, too."

Reuben slowed the car to a stop near the Jennings mailbox. "We'll see, Laurie. But don't mention it to Jenny. We wouldn't want to disappoint her if it couldn't be worked out."

He opened the door. "Well, come on girls. If you want to be first class dulcimer players, there's work to be done."

"I hope nobody's tired of fried chicken," Miss Polly said as she and her twelve guests walked into the lamplit dining room.

"Tired!" Keith exclaimed. "Man! I never ate before I came to Chestnut Lodge."

Mrs. Jennings laughed. "Chestnut Lodge was famous for the table it set, wasn't it Miss Polly?"

Miss Polly beamed. "It's almost like old times, I must say."

Keith, who had already made up his mind to see if Jenny would be interested in swapping dulcimer lessons for guitar lessons, turned to her. "I guess this place is as new to you as it is to me, isn't it?"

"Oh yes. It was closed before I was even born," Jenny replied.

Tom Sadd looked surprised. "Closed since before you were born! Why would a beautiful place like this ever have been closed?"

Reuben Kinkaid laughed almost too heartily. "Tom, mountain folk are like everybody else in these United States. They take notions to move on. Aunt Polly moved on. I coaxed her to come back."

Tom shook his head. "Seems to me if I had a place like this, I wouldn't move on as far as the nearest grocery store. It's so *apart* here."

"It sure is," Keith laughed. "In fact I was thinking of moving on a little closer—as far as the nearest square dance. It's tomorrow night in Honeybee, and how about you and Jenny coming with Laurie and me?" He turned to Jenny. "May I have the pleasure of the first Possum Trot, Miss Jennings?"

Jenny dimpled. "You may, Mr. Partridge, that is, if you'll play your guitar tonight. I'm about tired out on the dulcimer. I—" She broke off as a terrible snarling, wailing screech rent the air.

"Sakes," Miss Polly gasped as the weird cry died

44

away. "I haven't heard a painter in these mountains these many years!"

"A painter?" Chris asked in a shaky voice. "It sounded more like an animal to me."

"Painter is just another word for panther," Mr. Jennings explained. "Painter, panther, puma, cougar, catamount—they're all the same. Mountain lions."

Reuben nodded. "I've never heard one in my life. Just heard *about* them. I thought panthers had been killed off to the last one in these parts."

Shirley, white-faced, looked toward Reuben. "Well, that settles it! I'm not going to have the children roaming these trails if a mountain lion is on the prowl!"

Miss Polly leaned forward. "Mrs. Partridge, there's no need for worry on that score. Why, sakes! I'd doubt if they'd get a glimpse of that big cat if they were to set out on purpose looking for it."

Mr. Jennings nodded. "Maybe the best proof of that is the fact that nobody around here would find it easy to believe we even *heard* one tonight. I can tell you—the threat of the panther here is nothing compared to the threat of the gypsy moth."

Tom Sadd shivered. "I'd rather meet a gypsy moth face to face anyday."

"Not to change the subject," Mrs. Jennings said hastily, "but if Jenny is to go square dancing tomorrow night, we'd better call for her here afterwards. It's about impossible to back out and head down the road again at our place after dark."

"Fine!" Miss Polly crowed. "We'll have watermelon on the porch and pass the time nice as you please."

Danny suddenly spoke up. "You know what I just noticed? There're thirteen people at this table."

45

Reuben Kinkaid wagged his head. "Danny, that's certainly jolly! You're a great mathematician, but you are sure going to have to practice if you ever want to be the life-of-the-party."

Everybody, including Danny, laughed—everybody but Tom Sadd. He stared into the black night beyond the windows, and once again he shivered.

Chapter 5

☐ "What's the plan for today, boys?" Miss Polly asked, stepping out into the morning sunshine.

Tom grinned. "Now that I'm a man with a job, I was just about to ask for some time off, that is, if Keith would drive me down to Honeybee. I'd like to pick up some shirts and stuff. And," he tilted up a heavy hiking shoe, "if I'm going dancing tonight I'd better wear something besides these clodhoppers."

"That seems sensible. Permission granted," Miss Polly said. "Are Danny and Chris going with you?"

Keith laughed. "If you can believe it, they're not. Danny discovered some books on rocks in the lobby bookcases, and they're upstairs doing scientific research—about an hour's worth, I guess."

Reuben came out on the porch. "I see we're getting a second visit from Officer Clingley and his partner." He motioned toward the police cruiser just turning in the drive.

"Morning," Officer Clingley called as he pulled up to

a stop. "Morning, Miss Polly. Just thought we'd stop by and tell you they haven't given up on the skyjacker search. You'll probably see a good many searchers up here during the day. They're going farther upstream than they did yesterday."

"Upstream?" Reuben Kinkaid looked surprised.

Officer Clingley nodded. "You see they've figured that with the skyjacker making his jump almost at dawn, and the boys spotting the chute hours later, that there's a chance maybe he came down in the shallow water up there. Who knows? Maybe his chute dragged him into deep water. But maybe he dropped the money bag. Anyhow, the searchers will try to find some trace of what happened. The chute could have hung up on rocks along the way, a dozen times. That would account for the time difference."

Miss Polly shuddered. "I certainly hope this will soon be over. Thank you for stopping by, Lyle."

"Say, you men haven't met Tom Sadd, have you?" Reuben asked. "Come over here, Tom, and get yourself introduced. Maybe the officers can tell you how to go about getting a temporary drivers' license." Reuben turned to Officer Clingley. "Tom had a little misadventure yesterday."

As the officers shook hands with Tom, Reuben explained that Tom had been hired by Miss Polly to "help out" for a while.

Tom glanced down at his hiking boots. "I kind of hate to explain what my 'misadventure' was," he grinned, "after hearing Miss Polly's opinion of it."

Officers Clingley and Smith heard the story and burst out laughing. "I can't blame Miss Polly!" Officer Smith gasped. "A whole bicycle for one single little old copperhead? Man! You sure were using a cannon where a pea-shooter would have done the job better."

Tom laughed too. "Well, I told you I didn't want to tell it. I was just going down to Honeybee now for some replacements."

Officer Clingley laughed. "I can see that business in Honeybee is going to be looking up now that Miss Polly's back at Chestnut Lodge. By the way, Tom, it's just routine, but we'd better check your identification."

Tom groaned. "I don't have any. You see . . ." he began.

Reuben quickly explained. "Show him your traveler's checks, Tom. They'll do until you have something better."

"Sure they will," Officer Smith said. As Officer Smith glanced at the checkbook, Reuben Kinkaid said, "Almost forgot to tell you fellows—we have a panther up this way."

Officer Clingley's jaw dropped. "You're kidding! Even my pa only told stories *his* pa told about painters. Those cats are *mean*."

"Mean—and lonesome," Tom Sadd said. "At least the one we heard sure sounded lonesome to me."

"Lonesome!" Officer Smith laughed, handing back the checkbook. "Well, that's how I hope he stays—real lonesome. But we'll pass the word along to the State conservation people. That's going to be bigger news in these parts than the skyjacking."

All of Honeybee and half the county must have been at the square dance held in the Honeybee Opera House.

"I thought square dances were in barns," Laurie said, surprised, as Keith parked Reuben's convertible a block down the street from the Opera House.

"Not in Honeybee," Jenny laughed. "We don't have operas up this way so we might as well use the stage for the musicians and the floor for the dancers."

Keith switched off the motor. "Jenny, if I step on your feet, just yell. I don't know too much about square dances."

"Same here," Tom said. "Jenny, you'll have to steer us around."

"Count on me," Jenny grinned. "There's a square dance every Saturday night all summer, and I love them. Laurie, maybe Courtney Cross will be here next weekend. Just imagine! Wouldn't it be great?"

"Courtney Cross?" Laurie repeated in a slightly puzzled voice. "Oh, *him*."

As Keith opened the car door he shot a quick glance at his sister, and instantly he knew Laurie Partridge was in love again. Keith nearly groaned aloud. Tom Sadd was a perfectly nice guy, but a roving rock hunter, who had no more sense than to lose all his worldly possessions over Hairpin Bend, wasn't quite Keith's idea of a future brother-in-law.

Either Tom Sadd had been very modest about his talents as a square dancer, or he caught on quickly. Before the first "set" was over, he was expertly swinging Laurie to the quick, lively tunes of banjos and guitars and easily following the instructions sung out by the caller on the stage.

But while Laurie was having a wonderful time as she was whisked through the steps of a fast reel, Jenny was hard at work keeping Keith headed in the right direction.

"It's all this 'sashay right, sashay left,'" he panted at the end of the third dance. "Just when I get that figured out, there's a doh-si-doh. Wow! I'm a menace. I must have crashed into every girl on the floor."

"Don't worry," Jenny said. "They're all friends. And besides," she added tactfully, "no girl minds being bumped into when it's somebody famous."

"Thanks a lot," Keith said gloomily. "If I'm famous around here, it's going to be for knocking the wind out of half the girls in town."

Jenny exploded into laughter. She bent forward and tried to hide her face. "I . . . I'm sorry Keith," she gasped. "You're really a wonderful dancer . . . I can tell. It's just that—"

"—that when it comes to square dancing, I don't know my right foot from my left," Keith finished her sentence. "Oh man!" he groaned. "They're starting up again." He looked toward the stage where the caller was rapping for attention.

"Folks," the man at the mike called out, "it's been brought to my attention that we have two famous people here in Honeybee tonight—Keith Partridge and his sister, Laurie. And I'm wondering if they'd favor us with a tune? There's a spare guitar ready and waiting up here!"

A thunder of hand-clapping surged through the old Opera House. "Go ahead, Keith!" Jenny urged.

"Go ahead! Will I?" Keith grinned. "Man! I've never wanted to be on a stage so much in my life. Even if they don't like my playing style, at least everybody will be safe down here. Where's Laurie?"

51

Back at Chestnut Lodge everybody on the porch was listening to the late news on Danny's transistor radio.

"Aren't they ever going to tell us about the sky-jacker search?" Chris asked.

"It isn't big news now," Danny said. "After all, it happened three days ago."

"And now on to the latest news in the recent sky-jacking," the radio voice continued. "Late this afternoon searchers discovered a water-soaked jacket caught on the rocks upstream of Big Gorge. In it was a wallet positively identified as belonging to Elmer Tell of Buffalo, New York. This has led to the conclusion that Tell had been able to unharness his chute and get out of his jacket, but was unable to pull free of the strong river current before being caught in the turbulent waters downstream. No trace has been found of the airline's canvas bag containing $300,000. It is presumed that Elmer Tell clung to it even as he went to his death."

Shirley quickly stood up as Danny turned off the radio. "Miss Polly," she said hastily, "If Maribelle and Tracy would help serve, I'd be glad to cut the watermelon. Would you like me to?"

"Gladly, gladly," Miss Polly replied. "That's one of the best things about being eighty," she said. "You're very apt to have your watermelon cut for you."

As Shirley and the girls left for the kitchen, Miss Polly turned to Mr. Jennings. "No sooner do we hear the skyjacker is gone for sure, than we know a painter is here for sure."

"You haven't heard it again, have you?" Mr. Jennings asked.

52

Miss Polly shook her head. "No, but you know, it struck me all of a sudden that the thump I heard on the roof the other night—the night the Partridges first came, Reuben—was probably that big cat taking a shortcut down from a nearby tree."

"Don't tell Shirley, please, Aunt Polly," Reuben Kinkaid said. "You know how she'd worry about that."

"She sure would," Danny added. "Chris, we'd better never mention it, either."

Aunt Polly shook her head. "The funny thing to me is its getting so close to people. Sakes! I've heard them wail and screech. Years ago that was, but the cries were always far off."

"What's stranger to me is that there's a cat left to be heard, far off or close up. Everybody's thought they'd been hunted to extinction," Mr. Jennings said. He rapped his pipe on the porch railing. "I guess in the old days they were considered fair game. Say what you want about how they only killed a cow if they couldn't get a deer—it must have been a real worry to the man depending on a cow for milk and butter to feed his family, to know a panther might be depending on that same cow for meat."

"I've always heard they never would attack people unless they were cornered," Mrs. Jennings said. "So it must have turned into a cruel sport. If it hadn't, the panther population wouldn't be down to zero in these mountains."

"Zero minus one, don't forget," Danny said from the porch steps.

"Unless that cat's a mighty old bachelor, it's more likely to be zero minus two, or maybe five or six if there're kittens," Miss Polly replied. "That's what worries me."

"I don't see what you have to worry about, Miss Polly," Danny said cheerfully. "You don't have a cow. Do you know what's worrying me?"

"What's worrying you, sweetie," Shirley asked, opening the screen door for Maribelle and Tracy, who were carefully balancing plates of watermelon.

"I've got a strange feeling that Keith and Laurie are entertaining for free at that square dance."

"Danny!" his mother exclaimed.

"Well, if they'd told folks ahead of time, the square dance people could have charged extra and given the money to some worthy cause," Danny answered calmly.

"A *benefit* performance!" Tracy exclaimed. "Oh, Danny! You're smart!"

"Too smart," Reuben growled. "Laurie's under contract to Frameway Films right this minute."

"Keith isn't," Chris reminded Reuben.

Miss Polly spoke up. "As far as anybody knows, those young people are doing not a thing but doh-si-doh-ing, and that's the end of it."

"I just hope they don't doh-si-doh too long," Danny sighed. "We want to get an early start rock hunting tomorrow, and Keith forgot all about buying our hammers and stuff when he went to Honeybee today."

Miss Polly stopped creaking her rocker. "Hammers? Now why didn't I remember? There's no need to spend a penny on tools. Unless I'm very much mistaken, you'll find hammers and chisels a-plenty out in the old barn." She turned to the Jenningses. "I guess you remember when summer visitors up here used to hike around and come back loaded with rock samples? Quite a hobby it was."

Danny frowned. "You don't think the area is all mined out, do you, Miss Polly?"

"Sakes, no. If there's one thing not on the endangered list, it's the rocks in these mountains. You can even pick up some very nice crystals right along the roadsides between here and Honeybee."

Shirley looked out into the dark night. "There're the headlights. You're getting your wish, Danny. Here they come."

"So soon!" Danny exclaimed in a horrified voice. "Do you suppose they didn't get asked to perform?"

Everybody laughed. It was plain to see that The Partridge Family was one for all and all for one—even if they weren't all in the same movie.

Chapter 6

☐ In the morning when Danny and Chris came into the kitchen, Mrs. Griggs waved a hand toward the window. "You have to get up early to beat Miss Polly. She's had her breakfast and started out for the barn to get them rock chisels 'n' things."

"Thanks, Mrs. Griggs," Danny said. "Would you mind holding up on the scrambled eggs?"

"Run along," Mrs. Griggs smiled. "Reckon Miss Polly could use your help."

The boys slammed out the back door and raced toward the barn. "Miss Polly," Chris shouted, "here we come!"

"So I notice," Miss Polly shouted back. She chuckled. "I thought I was doing Reuben a real favor coming back up here, and I do believe he's done me a favor. I certainly like the Partridge family."

As the boys came puffing up, Miss Polly began to issue orders like a general. "First we lift this crossbar off. I'll take the middle and you boys get on the ends, and we'll all lift at once."

The cross bar was placed to one side of the big old double doors, and Miss Polly took a heavy old-fashioned key from her pocket. "We may need some oil," she said. "This padlock is mighty rusty."

But the key turned quite easily and the padlock swung free. "Now no rushing in," Miss Polly said. "It's black as pitch in there, I suspect, and goodness knows what we could stumble over. We'll push the doors wide open for as much daylight as possible."

Hardly were the doors swung back when a rush of air slapped at their nostrils—so strong, pungent and offensive that all three stepped back.

"Phew!" Danny gasped. "This place sure could use some fresh air."

Chris grabbed his nose and backed away. "Wow! Let's wait awhile."

"Wait awhile!" Miss Polly exclaimed. "Indeed we will. Heave the doors shut boys."

"*Shut.* How's it going to get aired out if the doors are shut?" Danny asked.

"Whew!" Miss Polly fanned her face. "Up with the bar, boys. Can you manage?"

Danny and Chris exchanged puzzled looks, but they heaved up the crossbar and dropped it into place.

"I should think you'd want to air the place," Chris said disapprovingly.

Miss Polly didn't reply. "Let's get straight away, boys," she said, marching back toward the lodge.

As the boys caught up with her, Miss Polly paused and looked back at the old building. "Boys, didn't that smell remind you of anything?" she asked.

"How could it?" Danny asked. "I never smelled a smell like that in my whole life."

"And you Chris?" Miss Polly asked.

Chris hesitated. "Well, maybe something like cats. I mean, if you didn't keep the place cleaned up for them."

Miss Polly nodded. "Cats," she said grimly. "And unless I'm very much mistaken, from the way that old barn smells, that panther we heard the other night must have denned up there for goodness knows how many years."

"You mean a panther right *in the backyard?*" Danny asked excitedly. "Man, we'd better tell the sheriff or something, somebody who has a gun."

Miss Polly looked sharply at Danny. "My goodness! A gun! According to all I've been hearing, it's *my* generation who were the exterminators. Looks like you haven't been taking this ecology talk seriously after all."

Danny flushed. "Well, you don't want a panther this close, do you?"

"No, I don't," Miss Polly said briskly. "And now that I think about it, there's little danger that it's anywhere close now. Even in the old days they were right solitary in their ways. And what with people up here opening summer cabins, and all the new places built too, that panther is long gone—probably holed up in a den atop the mountain. But I don't want to go back into that barn, couldn't stand the smell. I reckon you'd better go into Honeybee Hardware after all for the things you need for your adventures with Tom Sadd."

By the time they returned to the back porch, everybody was having breakfast—everybody but Tom.

Danny and Chris went to the kitchen for their scrambled eggs and bacon. "I sure thought Tom wouldn't sleep late," Chris said, grumbling.

"He didn't sleep late," Mrs. Griggs said. "He was first up. I packed him a couple of sandwiches and a thermos of coffee, and away he went."

"*Went*. Where?"

Mrs. Griggs reached into her apron pocket. "Here. He left this note for you."

"Dear Dan and Chris," Danny read as Chris looked over his shoulder. "I might as well look around for a good place to start our rock hunting. Thought I'd use the time while you pick up the following at the hardware. That way, no time will be lost. Here it is: chisels, hammers, white tiles (these are for color streaking—will explain that later), small notebooks, broad adhesive tape (for sticking on specimens temporarily), ballpoint pens for marking adhesive labels, and, important, some work gloves. Back before noon. Thanks, Tom.

P.S. Tell the hardware man you're going to hunt rocks. He'll know the right size tools you'll need to buy. Maybe you'd better get a small plastic pail for carrying water (for rinsing off rocks, not for drinking purposes). Will pay my share later."

"Well—I guess that's sensible," Chris said slowly. "But it would have been more fun if we'd started looking for a place together."

"That's the thing about people as they get older," Danny sighed. "They keep on getting more sensible all the time. Oh well, let's eat and tell Keith we'll have to get this stuff after breakfast."

Trays in hand, the boys reached the porch doorway just as the telephone rang in the lobby.

"Now who would be calling this early in the day?" Miss Polly asked, putting down her coffee cup and rising.

"Not Frameway Films, anyhow," Reuben Kinkaid said as Miss Polly trotted briskly off to the lobby. "It's not even morning in California."

Danny and Chris sat down. "Did Miss Polly tell you about the panther in the barn?" Chris asked.

Under the table, Danny's sneaker shot out in a fast clip on Chris's ankle as Shirley gasped, "Panther in the barn!"

"He's being dramatic, Mom," Danny answered. "It just used to be in the barn. Miss Polly says that now it's summer and people are around, it's moved farther up the mountain."

Shirley looked worried. "Honestly, boys, everything seems so dangerous. I want you to promise me you won't go wandering off on your own away from Tom or Keith."

"Tom's wandered away from us," Chris said. "He's gone to look for a good place for us to hunt rocks, so we're supposed to go down to Honeybee Hardware. Will you take us, Keith?"

"Sure," Keith answered, yawning. "Just give me a chance to wake up first, will you?"

Miss Polly came back to the porch. "That was a Mr. Harris from Frameway Films calling," she said. "I told him you were at breakfast, Reuben, and that you would call him back."

Reuben groaned. "Aunt Polly, now why didn't you

call me to the phone? I might as well have talked to California on his nickel."

"Oh, he wasn't calling from California," Aunt Polly replied. "He called direct from the Honeybee Hotel. He said for you to call back as soon as possible as they're all set to go—which struck me as very odd considering they just arrived."

Danny nearly spluttered his orange juice, and Reuben Kinkaid quickly rose from the table. "Maybe he meant Frameway Films is all set to go to work," he said, keeping a straight face. "I'll call now and find out for sure."

"I can tell you one thing," Laurie Partridge sighed as Reuben left the porch. "I'm not ready to play the dulcimer, Mom. And I think Jenny's just about given up trying to teach me, and there will go my big chance."

"I wouldn't worry, dear," Shirley said comfortingly. "Just because the movie people are here now, doesn't mean they'll start shooting right away."

Danny stole a quick look at Aunt Polly. "Mom means cameras, not guns, Miss Polly."

She eyed him sternly. "Young man, I wasn't born yesterday," she replied. Then she suddenly chuckled. "Not to say that comes as any surprise to you, I daresay."

Reuben Kinkaid came hurrying back to the porch. "Aunt Polly," he asked, "How're we set for groceries? I've invited Mr. Harris to come up here for dinner tonight. That makes three extra. Do you want me to pick up anything in Honeybee?"

"Wait a minute, Mr. Kinkaid," Danny said. "Mr. Harris makes one extra."

Reuben frowned. "One? Oh! Well, he's bringing Alison Park and Courtney Cross. They're playing the lead roles, you know. That makes three."

At the same time, Laurie gasped, "Courtney Cross!", Keith exclaimed, "Alison Park! Oh wow!" and Shirley said, "Mr. Harris? I've *always* wanted to meet him."

Aunt Polly chuckled. "Mrs. Griggs and I like nothing more than a party, so don't you worry about a thing, Reuben. We'll manage nicely."

"And Laurie and I will help too," Shirley said.

"Not this morning," Reuben said hastily. "Dulcimer lessons as usual. I'll drop you off at Jennings, but Keith will have to pick you up at noon. I don't know just when I'll get back."

Danny and Chris groaned. "But Mr. Kinkaid, Keith's supposed to come rock hunting with us as soon as Tom gets back," Danny said.

"Don't worry, Danny," Shirley laughed. "We'll hike back. It will do us good."

Laurie groaned and Danny hurriedly jumped to his feet. "Let's go to Honeybee for our stuff now, Keith, or we may never get started. We'd better go before anything else happens here—like Laurie spraining her toe, or something, so she can't walk."

"With the rocks you have in your head, Daniel Partridge, I'm wondering why you're going out looking for more," Laurie said icily.

But before Tom Sadd finally returned, Danny was almost sure something else *had* happened. "Maybe he's got himself lost," he said worriedly.

63

"Or maybe, broken his leg," Chris suggested gloomily.

"Or stepped on a rattlesnake," Danny added.

"Or run into that panther," Chris frowned.

"It's a good thing Mom isn't here to hear you talk that way or nobody would be going anywhere," Keith grinned. "But you can stop worrying. Here he comes now." He waved his hand toward the path that led down from Big Gorge.

Tom came striding toward the porch. "All set?" he called.

"All *set*. Man, we thought maybe you weren't ever coming back," Danny called back.

As Tom came up the steps, Keith spoke up. "Say, you aren't planning to go back along the gorge, are you, Tom? We sort of promised Miss Polly that we'd stay away from there."

Tom shook his head. "Oh, I know her feelings about that place by now, Keith. No, I took a back trail, and it came out way above the gorge. Up there, the river's only about a foot deep, and it's a great place to look around. We can go up and back the same way, so Miss Polly won't need to be worried about us."

"Well let's start!" Chris exclaimed. "First thing you know, it'll be afternoon. I never heard of a business that waits to get started after lunch, for goodness sake!"

Chapter 7

☐ "There's one good thing about rock hunting," Chris puffed as he and Danny climbed the uphill trail behind Keith and Tom.

"What?" Danny puffed back.

"You don't have to carry a lot of junk like if you were going on safari."

Danny shook his head. "It's the trip back that's tough—after you've found the rocks."

Tom Sadd slowed down and looked back at the hikers. "Anybody want to take a break?" he called.

"How much farther is it?" Danny asked.

"Maybe ten minutes."

"Ten minutes!" Chris promptly sat down right in the middle of the trail, and Danny dropped down beside him.

"There's your answer, Tom." Keith mopped at his forehead. "Those rocks you're taking us to had better be good. How far have we come, anyhow?"

"Not so far—about two miles, I guess. Why?"

Keith headed for a low, flat boulder at the side of

the trail. He sat down and looked over at the panting Danny and Chris. "Maybe for the first day we should have planned more hunting and less hiking," he said. "The kids are going to be tired out before they start."

Tom frowned. "I guess I forgot about you people not being in training for this sort of thing. Oh, well. We don't have to go back to the lodge on this trail. We can just follow the river—that's not half this distance. Probably Miss Polly won't even notice which way we come back."

Keith sighed. "Can't. The kids and I made a sort of pact with Miss Polly not to use that path. I guess we're stuck with the long way home."

"Nobody has to step into the gorge, but it's up to you," Tom said shortly. "I'm not the one who minds a little hike." He stood up. "Let's get started."

But Keith leaned back on his elbows. "Okay." He looked steadily at Tom. "But tell me something first. We've passed only about a million rocks. Why drag the kids along and make a big thing about hunting along the river? Why didn't you just say it, Tom? You want to look for the airlines money."

Tom's dark brows drew tight together. Then suddenly he laughed. "I'll have to sit down again for this. You have the questions, and I have the answers." He called over to Chris and Danny. "Hey, kids—come over here. I'm going to make a speech."

Tom lost no time in what he had to say. "Keith's asked me some questions, and I thought you'd like to know the answers, too. First, he wants to know why we came such a long way when there are plenty of rocks around the lodge. Then he asked if looking for the airline's money wasn't the real reason for going as far as the river." He paused. "It was. I thought we might as well take our turn—everybody else has—looking for those missing three-hundred thousand bucks the skyjacker may have dropped. But I didn't want to tell you that because then you'd just have your eyes open for a canvas bag. And if you didn't see it right along the river banks you might think it just might be hidden in a rhododendron thicket. And going into a thicket would be a good way to get lost. Anyhow, whether we find the money or not, we're going to find some good rock specimens."

Danny's eyes gleamed. "Let's go!" he exclaimed.

"Wait a minute," Tom said. "There's one thing Keith didn't ask—why I'd try to find the money when there's already been a search." He looked at Keith and grinned. "I have two pretty good reasons. One, is that what with my bike gone and my traveler's checks nearly gone, I sure wouldn't mind getting a reward from the airlines. And two, I have a hunch."

Danny's eyes widened. "A hunch? What about?"

Tom hesitated. "I've given this a lot of thought," he said. "Everybody seems to figure that the skyjacker *may* have dropped the money, but that he went down in the gorge for *sure*. But I began thinking—what if he came down *beside* the river? It's so stony along here, there wouldn't be a footprint to show where he landed. Maybe he got out of his chute harness, hid it, and began walking downstream heading for civilization. Then he'd see the gorge, and that would give him an idea. Why not go back and get his chute? Then purposely, he'd throw it and his jacket into the river. That way, they'd either be lost forever, or if they were found, everybody would think he was dead. Then all he'd have to do would be to hide the money and come back for it after all the excitement had died down."

"Man!" Danny breathed. "That isn't a hunch, it's a *theory*. I'm sure glad you brought us along."

Chris leaned close to Keith's knee. "But maybe the skyjacker is still around," he said in a small voice. "And he wouldn't like it so much if he saw us looking for rocks."

Keith looked at Danny's eager face. "Looking for rocks means looking for rocks. That means you don't stick your hands somewhere that looks like a hiding place. You might find a snake instead of a canvas bag."

"I could use a stick," Danny said thoughtfully.

Tom burst out laughing. "What's happened to Danny Partridge, scientist and business man? Are you giving up the rock business before you even get started? I'll tell you what, Danny, let me do the money hunting, and I'll promise a four-way split on the reward."

"You *would!*" Danny exclaimed, astonished. "Tom, you sure need a business manager is all I can say. How about three parts to you and one part to the Partridges? That's only good sense."

Tom reached out his hand and touched Danny's red hair. "Okay, business manager," he laughed. "Now let's get going. Okay, Keith?"

"Okay," Keith grinned.

Even if they didn't come back loaded with the emeralds, rubies, and sapphires that Chris was hoping to

68

find, the mountain stream was almost worth the long hike. It splashed icily along, and beneath its shallow waters, pebbles shone and glittered in the sunlight.

For all the talk about a lost three-hundred thousand dollars, Keith noticed that Chris and Danny seemed to have forgotten everything but exploring for rocks.

"You see," Tom was saying as he bent over a small rock outcrop at the edge of the stream, "the whole crust of the world is made up of rock. Even the soil on farms is rock—ground up fine as fine. And rocks are made up of minerals, and minerals are made of elements. It's a big study and we're sort of beginning in the middle. Now take this—." With chisel and hammer he clinked at the rock at his feet until a small chunk split off. "See?"

Chris, Danny and Keith all leaned forward.

"It just looks like rock to me," Chris said disappointedly. "I thought the insides would be more sparkly."

"Or have some beautiful design," Danny added. "Honest, Tom, do you think you picked a good rock?"

Tom handed a small chunk to Danny. "Go wash it off in the water, Danny. See if it makes any difference."

Danny swished it in the mountain stream. "Well not a lot," he said. "It's a little prettier, I guess."

"Wait until you see it polished," Tom replied. "And of course, it has to be shaped, too."

"What is it?" Chris asked.

"Olivine. When you come across a very clear, glassy specimen, it can be cut into gem peridot. That's a very beautiful green stone."

"I'd rather find a very beautiful green emerald, myself," Danny said.

"And I'd like to find rubies," Chris announced. "Let's get to work."

Not only was it a "big study," as Tom had said, it was finger-blistering work. And it wasn't long before Chris and Danny put down their chisels and hammers and began gathering small stones and bright pebbles from the bed of the mountain stream.

"How'd it be if we collect these and sort them out when we get back to the lodge, Tom?" Danny asked. "We just might happen to pick up something valuable."

Tom nodded. "Good idea. And I'll keep on along the bank upstream. If I come across something interesting, I'll holler. Want to come with me, Keith?"

Keith shook his head. "Do you know what I'm going to do? Take off my shoes. You go on ahead."

As the two younger boys waded in the broad, shallow stream, Keith propped himself comfortably against a mossy boulder. Lazily he watched Tom make his way upstream, stopping every now and then to bend over and examine something. "It would be great if he could find that money," Keith thought. "I wish I hadn't said what I did. I sure must have sounded like a . . . well, like a guy who never has to worry about where his next bicycle is coming from. Why shouldn't he want to get some dough? He doesn't have much of a job, either—even if it was nice of Miss Polly to sort of take him in after he lost all his gear. I'm going to think of something we could do for him," he thought sleepily. "Something nice."

Keith's eyes blinked as sunlight glinted on the water. He stood up, spotted a flat boulder, and stretched out on it, turning his head toward the deep green undergrowth beyond the river bank. "This is better," he thought sleepily.

His eyelids drooped, fluttered open, then drooped again, narrowing to slits. Not five feet away from him, two shoes and trouser legs moved—slowly, quietly, until they were completely out of sight in the heavy thicket.

Across the stream, Danny and Chris had climbed up to the bank and were sorting out their loot.

"Do you know what, Dan?" Chris said disgustedly. "We didn't bring anything to carry our rock specimens back in."

"We can use our t-shirts," Danny said calmly.

"Mine isn't so big," Chris answered unhappily. "And look at all this stuff I have already."

"Use Keith's shirt. He's not using it for anything. He isn't even moving. I think he's asleep. See?" He waved his arm in Keith's direction.

"Well, I'm going back and wake him up," Chris said. "Before I collect more stuff, I'd better make arrangements with him in advance."

He peeled off his t-shirt and piled the stones in it. "See you on the other side," he said, bundling the shirt into a package and fitting it under his arm.

"Okay," Danny answered, almost absent-mindedly. "I'm going to do some sorting right now in case I have doubles of anything."

Chris had reached the other side of the stream before Danny was ready to knot his shirt into a bundle. "What I need is a stick," he thought. He looked behind him toward the dense woods and undergrowth. Almost

71

right away, he spotted a broken branch caught among the foliage. "Just what I need," he thought.

Pulling the branch free was harder than he'd expected. He gave it a few strong yanks. Suddenly it swung free, and Danny's feet shot out from under him. He fell backwards, quickly rolled over on his stomach, and it was from ground level that he made the discovery of the day—a glint of gold catching the sunlight. Amazed, he wriggled forward and closed his hand over—a safety razor! As he jerked it free of the underbrush, something dragged with it, and for a second Danny nearly jumped to his feet and ran. Then he edged closer. "Ugh! It must be a dead animal!" he muttered. Using the razor as a drag, he cautiously turned over the dark, hairy mass and could hardly believe his eyes. "It's a wig!" he gasped. "Man! Wait until Tom sees this. It proves his hunch was right. The skyjacker landed safe and sound. He just shaved off his beard and took off his wig. Man! Nobody knows what Elmer Tell really looked like, I guess."

Hurriedly, he unknotted the t-shirt and dropped his find into it. Then, forgetting all about using the branch as a carrying pole, Danny hastily set out for the opposite bank.

But as he waded along, he had second thoughts about telling Tom about his discovery. "I'd better not say anything," he decided. "Chris would be sure to think the skyjacker would jump us on the way back."

He looked toward the dark shadows of the opposite bank, and in spite of the warm sunshine midstream, he shivered. "I hope Tom is right," he muttered. "I hope that guy is miles from here."

By the time the rock hunters reached the lodge steps even Tom Sadd wasn't striding along as fast as he usually did, and Chris was hobbling.

Shirley Partridge leaned over the porch railing. "Thank goodness!" she exclaimed. "I was beginning to wonder if you'd be back in time to clean up for dinner."

Danny sighed as he dropped down on the steps. "When Columbus got home," he said, "I suppose the first thing Queen Isabella said was, 'Columbus, get right into the tub. The royal dinner is on the table.'"

Keith laughed as he dropped down beside Danny. "Just for that, don't show her the treasures of the New World, Danny."

"For goodness sake, boys," Shirley implored. "Don't sit down. Mr. Harris and the others will be here in no time, and there's only one bathtub around here, if you remember."

Danny grinned. "Don't worry, Mom. They'll probably take baths before they get here."

"Very funny," Shirley managed to say sternly, right in the middle of a giggle. She glanced at Chris who was slowly limping up the steps. "What's wrong with your foot?"

Chris sat down on the step and pulled off his sneaker and sock.

"Chris!" his mother exclaimed. "That heel's raw! My goodness, how far did you boys walk? Keith, how could you have *let* him?"

Tom spoke up quickly. "It's my fault, Mrs. Partridge. Why didn't you say something, Chris? I would have carried you."

Chris's face turned red. "I'm a little old to ride piggyback," he said stiffly. "Or to be *let*, either, Mom. Besides, it doesn't hurt now that I can wave it around in the air."

"Well, you're going to have to wave it around in a footbath," his mother said. "You take your bath first while I see if Miss Polly has a dishpan we can borrow."

She followed Chris into the lodge, then turned back at the door. "You're on next, Keith. We've invited Jenny Jennings, too. And I told her you'd call for her around six-thirty. Nobody dawdle, please." She slammed the door.

Danny stood up. "Well, you guys can use my turn in the tub," he said. "I'll use the bird bath."

"What's that?"

"The wash bowl in the bedroom," Danny replied, marching off.

Keith chuckled. "Wait until Mom hears that. Danny's living in a dream world. Mom's a great believer in baths."

Tom looked thoughtful. "You know, if Mr. Kinkaid was willing to spend a little money, I could rig up an outdoor shower below the bathroom window. It sure could get a lot of use around here."

Keith looked surprised. "Tom, you certainly have a lot of talents—writing, rock hunting, and now plumbing. What else?"

Tom laughed. "I'm pretty good with horses, too. Maybe we could take Miss Polly's suggestion about going riding, that is, if anyone is interested."

"Sure. Laurie would love it. She's the big horse enthusiast of the family." Keith suddenly sat up. "And what about Courtney Cross? In his pictures he's always galloping somewhere."

"And Alison Park," Tom added. "Say, this idea is getting better all the time. And Jenny, maybe she'd be interested. She probably knows all the trails around here."

"Jenny!" Keith jumped up. "I'd better get going. It's nearly six o'clock. See you later."

Tom watched Keith stride off into the lodge. Slowly he stood up and looked across the quiet mountains and the valley below. He suddenly shivered. Another picture had come into his mind—not soft smoky blue mountains, but the heavy paw prints by a sandy upstream stretch along the river bank. "That cat was *there*," he shuddered. "I know it. Staring and watching and *waiting* for me, back there in the thickets." He turned on his heel and went into the lodge. "Don't be a fool," he muttered aloud.

Tom Sadd wasn't the only one having uncomfortable visions. Keith Partridge, sloshing about in the old-fashioned tub was wondering how he could call Officer Clingley without Miss Polly or the others knowing about it. It would ruin Danny's and Chris's vacation if their mother knew what Keith had seen as he lay by the stream bank.

"Man! She'd have us 'playing in the yard' for sure," he muttered. "But I'll have to call the State troopers."

Down the hall, the minute Chris hobbled off to Miss Polly's borrowed dishpan, Danny slid the old-fashioned lock-bolt on the bedroom door. Then quickly he unknotted his t-shirt and gingerly shook out the dark curly wig. He hesitated. Then walking to the mirror, Danny tried it on. "It's just like the guy on the radio said," he thought. "It sure does look like a shrub. I'd better tell Keith and Tom first chance I get, but I hope Mom won't have to know about it. She'd—"

The doorknob suddenly rattled and Keith called, "Hey, Danny. Open up."

Danny took a fast look in the mirror and tweaked the wig into a better position. "Okay," he called back, and hurrying to the door, stepped behind it as he swung it open.

"How come you locked—" Keith's eyes opened almost in horror. "Danny!"

Danny carefully closed and bolted the door. "It's only a wig," he said. "I mean, I haven't been in here growing it, or anything."

"Well take it off," Keith exclaimed. "You look like a . . . a *heap*. Where'd you get it?"

Danny twitched the dark mass off his head and tossed it on a chair. "It's the skyjacker's, I imagine," he said coolly. "And I found his safety razor, too. Look." He lifted it from the rock collection. "Tom's hunch was really right. I guess we'd better tell the police, hadn't we?"

"We sure had," Keith replied. "I'll do it right now."

Danny frowned. "Couldn't it wait until tomorrow?" he asked. "I mean everybody's around now, and you know how Mom is. She'll have us playing in the yard yet if she hears about this."

Keith shook his head. "Maybe we'd better," he said uneasily.

Danny stared. "You're kidding!"

"Well, what if Tom was only half right? Instead of being miles away, suppose the skyjacker was up there this afternoon and saw you take this stuff?" He thought a minute. "I'll tell you what, Danny. You get cleaned up as fast as you can, then get Mom out on the porch, or out of the lobby, anyhow, and I'll call the police."

"I've a better idea," Danny said. "I could go with you to pick up Jenny. We could use her phone, and maybe Officer Clingley would meet us there. That way, Miss Polly wouldn't get all upset seeing a police car and everything."

Keith grinned. "Miss Polly? You mean Mom, don't you? Okay. But Danny, no bird bath. Wash your hair while you're at it. Ugh!"

Chapter 8

☐ It was nearly eight o'clock before Keith and Danny returned with Jenny. Miss Polly promptly led her guests into the dining-room.

As Mr. Harris pulled out her chair, Miss Polly chirped, "For a time, I didn't think Danny and Chris would be with us for dinner. They've had a strenuous day of rock hunting, haven't you boys?"

"Rock hunting?" Mr. Harris's face lighted up. "I'm an old rock hound myself. I'd forgotten, but this is just the country for it, isn't it? Did you get any good specimens?"

"Tom is our expert," Keith answered, pushing Jenny's chair forward. "In fact, he came up here to do a magazine article on rock hunting. But he had a little accident that side-tracked him."

"Tom's bad luck turned into our good luck," Shirley smiled. "He's been showing the boys the ins and outs of rock hunting."

"Too many ins and outs, I guess," Tom said ruefully. "Chris will have to stay off that foot for awhile, I'm afraid."

Chris's sleepy eyes suddenly widened. "You mean I can't go tomorrow?" he burst out. "But that isn't fair, Mom. We're a business—the Partridge Family Rocks, Inc. We're going to sell them."

Mr. Harris looked interested. "Then why don't you handle the selling end, just for awhile. Every business needs a business man."

"I'm the business man," Danny said quickly. "Chris is more of a scientist."

"I am?" Chris asked, surprised.

"Sure. You're a better reader than I am," Danny replied.

"Oh, that." Chris's face fell.

Mr. Harris looked quickly from one boy to the other. "If that's the case, Chris, maybe you could let me work with you in identifying the rocks."

Chris glowed. "I guess I could," he said shyly. He turned to Shirley. "Oh wow, Mom. I didn't think I'd be the one a big Hollywood director wanted to work with!"

By the time dinner was over, Miss Polly had plainly fallen in love with Mr. Harris. "No wonder he can tell people what to do in a movie," she thought. "He sees deep inside everybody."

She arose from the table. "Ladies, shall we take the air on the verandah and leave the gentlemen to their conversation?"

Before Tracy could ask Miss Polly what they would do with the air after they took it, Shirley Partridge quickly spoke up. "Miss Polly, may Danny and Chris be excused? I think they're ready to say goodnight."

"Certainly," Miss Polly nodded. "And Tracy, too, if she wishes."

"I wasn't rock-hunting," Tracy said gloomily. "I was just playing with Maribelle Jennings. I want to take the air too."

Alison Park laughed and put her arm around the little girl. "You know, I have a sister just about your age, Tracy. She's at home in California."

Courtney Cross, who had been very quiet all during dinner, smiled. "Alison always has—"

Nobody was to hear what Alison Park always had. A sudden screeching wail rent the air and sent Courtney Cross leaping out of his chair. "What was *that!*" he exclaimed.

"Our panther," Danny said calmly. "He screeched that way the other night when there was company for dinner. There were thirteen of us then, like tonight."

Alison Park glanced nervously at Courtney Cross. "Bad luck," she whispered.

Reuben Kinkaid flushed red. "Danny, you know what I said about learning to be the life-of-the-party?"

Danny sighed. "I guess I'm just too much of a statistician to ever be popular." He turned to Mr. Harris. "A statistician is one who gathers facts," he said helpfully.

"Danny, Miss Polly said you were excused," Keith said in a low voice. "Why don't you go gather facts —*in private.*"

Danny yawned. "Okay." He stood up with Chris. "And remember, everybody, for some people 13 is a very lucky number."

Later, when Shirley returned from tucking in Tracy for the night, Jenny Jennings was plucking the first sweet notes from her dulcimer.

"Give us a lively tune, Jenny," Miss Polly was saying. *Old Dan Tucker*—that's lively."

Jenny nodded and thrummed the first chords. Her voice rose true and clear.

Back in the shadows, Keith watched and listened. "If Mom and Miss Polly were purposely trying to sabotage Laurie's movie career, they couldn't have done better," he thought. "Jenny has the looks and the voice and the right accent for that part in the movie, and Mr. Harris isn't missing a thing. Poor Laurie!"

"My! How that music does take me back," Miss Polly sighed, as the tune ended.

Mr. Harris asked if he might look at the dulcimer. "Of course," Jenny replied, handing it to him. "They aren't like the dulcimers they wrote about in the Bible, you know, or like the ones they had in Europe. They're played with little hammers or sticks. These are sort of skinny violins, and you pluck them instead of using a bow. This one has just four strings. It was made by my great grandfather way back when. I guess mountain people made them to suit themselves, because they're not all alike."

"It has a sweet tone," Keith said.

"Keith, why don't you get your guitar," Jenny suggested.

"Sure, if Laurie will sing with me," he answered, hoping Laurie wouldn't say something dumb like "I couldn't possibly, not after hearing Jenny."

But Laurie hadn't even heard her brother. Tucked up in a corner of the porch swing, she was looking from Courtney Cross to Tom Sadd. "Courtney's terribly handsome," she thought. "I thought I'd simply collapse if he even said hello to me. But there's something about Tom. I don't know. He's like his name—sad. He never mentions a family, or anything. There's something so lonesome about him. And I like him. I like him a lot."

Keith was back, guitar in hand. "Before I forget," he said, "is anybody interested in horseback riding tomorrow besides Laurie and Tom and me? How about you, Court, and Alison and Jenny?"

Alison Park laughed. "You'll never get me on a horse. They scare me to death."

Jenny giggled. "I'm certainly glad you said that, Alison. It gives me courage." She looked up at Keith. "I know the trails, though, and if you get Mr. MacFarlane to promise me a very elderly, nice old horse, I'd go."

Courtney Cross looked over at Mr. Harris. "I'd like to get in some riding. Would it be okay with you?"

"Ride away," Mr. Harris smiled. "The crew will be doing footage only for the gorge scenes tomorrow, so the day is your own."

The evening sped by as Laurie and Keith took turns with Jenny in singing, and Shirley too joined in.

"There's one more song I'd like to hear," Miss Polly said. "Jenny, could you play *Fly Around My Pretty Little Miss* or *Foggy Mountain Top*?" She turned to Mr. Harris. "They're old tunes, real mountain music. Maybe it would be nice if you had them in your movie."

Lightly, Jenny's fingers plucked the strings. Miss Polly closed her eyes, leaned back, and not until Jenny touched the last chord did she open them. "I knew a girl who sounded just like that, and she played that very dulcimer—your grandmother Jenny."

"That sounds just like the plot of the movie!" Alison Park exclaimed.

Miss Polly creaked her rocker. "I hope not," she said. "The girl I knew came to a very terrible end. Oh, she was no girl by that time," she went on. "Sixty, she must have been."

"What happened?" Alison asked.

Jenny spoke up quickly. "It's a sad, old story. Maybe Miss Polly would rather not think anymore about it."

Miss Polly shook her head. "No. I guess your music has brought it all to mind—that, and making the movie here. Maybe I *should* tell it, Mr. Harris, just to give fair warning about Big Gorge."

Not a rocker creaked as Miss Polly began her story.

"It all happened a long time ago. Twenty years ago, to be exact. If Danny were here, he'd say, 'Miss Polly, you must have been sixty,' and he'd be just about right.

"At any rate, that summer it seemed that quite a few friends of years gone by were home visiting Honeybee folks. Of course, some of us had never left —like Jenny's grandma and me. One afternoon she said to me, 'Why don't we plan a kind of reunion party, Polly?'

"At first we thought we'd arrange for it to be at the new Honeybee High School. Then we thought that wouldn't be like old times at all. So Jenny wanted to have it here at Chestnut Lodge. I said I thought a picnic by the gorge would be more fun, and I argued for that. Well, the idea caught on, and what with husbands and wives it was going to be quite a crowd—twenty-three of us."

Miss Polly came to a dead stop. Nobody spoke.

"Well," she began again, "cars began arriving from Honeybee and everybody gathered. Finally, off we started on foot along the gorge path. We were all loaded down with picnic baskets and pillows and things like that.

"We'd no more reached the fork where one path goes up and one cuts straight across to the gorge, when I remembered that I hadn't picked up the little basket in the kitchen—you know, the important one with things in it like salt and pepper and mustard and can openers.

"I gave the basket I was carrying to Homer Berry. 'I'll just scamper back,' I said. 'It won't take me long to catch up again!' So Homer went on."

Miss Polly swallowed. "It was to be the last time I'd see him, or any of those friends of my girlhood. I scampered back all right. I was hurrying along the path, when all of a sudden there was a noise like thunder—a heavy, booming sound, and I heard dreadful cries. I ran to the clearing. There were the table-cloths spread out and the picnic baskets weighting them down and there were the pillows. *But not a living soul in sight*. Nothing but the roar of the river in my ears.

"I ran up and down. Calling out, I was, for everybody. And then I *saw*."

Aunt Polly sighed heavily. "I saw the fresh split-off in the rock just above the whirlpool, and then I saw the broken rocks below. And right away, I knew what had happened. Everybody had gone to take a look at Big Gorge from the platform rock, a closeup look. When that big chunk broke away, it hurled them into the white water."

There was another pause. "Well, that was the end of the picnic and Chestnut Lodge, and almost of me. *I* was the one who'd argued for a picnic.

"One by one, and two by two, they were found downstream—those that weren't caught in the rock fall." She turned to Reuben. "Do you wonder I call it 'killer gorge'? It's full of ghosts, for me."

Reuben didn't answer. Miss Polly turned to Mr. Harris. "A good deal is said about ecology and how things change. Does nobody think of change in the mountains? Wind and snow, fast water and rain. They all eat away at the earth itself. What's to prevent another such terrible break in the rocks? Think twice, Mr. Harris, before you must blame yourself, as I have, for taking people near that gorge."

Reuben Kinkaid's heart sank. "First the panther scares them to death. Next, Jenny proves she ought to have Laurie's part. And now Aunt Polly throws gloom and doom all over the place. We might as well pack our bags in the morning. This place is jinxed," he said to himself.

But to his relief, Mr. Harris was taking Miss Polly's story very calmly. "You're perfectly right, Miss Polly," he said. "And that's why we've had geologists scouting for rock fissures—anything that would be a danger to our crew or cast. But we won't be on location near the gorge. We'll camp upstream. In California, we did the scenes that would be inside a mountain cabin. And we've already had a scout out looking around for a good campsite."

Keith's eyebrows went up. "Maybe I saw a movie scout," he thought. "But why would a movie scout hide? No. It *must* have been the skyjacker."

Mr. Harris stood up. "You see, Miss Polly, we believe Americans should see, if only on film, how beautiful their country is. Maybe it will help them to want to keep its wilderness areas beautiful, and I think this picture will help. And now we must be going back to Honeybee. It's been a wonderful evening."

Chapter 9

☐ Miss Polly woke up in excellent spirits. "You know, Reuben," she said at the breakfast table, "It would have saved me a sight of worry if I'd known Mr. Harris's plans all along. He's a very nice man. Very sensible, too."

Reuben stirred his coffee and said nothing.

"And you know what I've been thinking?" Miss Polly went on. "Mr. Harris is right. Americans should have a chance to see their own country. I believe I shall will the gorge property to the United States as a national park.

Reuben nearly spilled his coffee cup. "What do you have in mind, Aunt Polly? A national mini-park?"

"What's that?"

"Short for 'miniature.' As national parks go, the gorge property isn't very big, you know."

"Maybe you're right." Miss Polly looked thoughtful. "I'll will it to the City of Honeybee, then. Of course I'd insist on their putting up proper safety devices. Meantime," she said briskly, "I hope you'll get busy and arrange for the Polly Kincaid College Scholarships. How many do you think I could give?"

Her nephew shook his head. "Aunt Polly, I've no head for figures this early in the day."

"That's all right," Miss Polly said cheerfully. "I'll ask Danny when he comes in for breakfast."

Her nephew sputtered coffee. "That kid!" he exclaimed. "Ask his advice and you might wind up with a new business manager, and you'd have to pay him."

Miss Polly laughed. She patted Reuben's arm. "And you're not angry with me about Jenny, are you?"

Reuben dropped his spoon and stared at his aunt's pink face. "You mean you *planned* it so Mr. Harris would want Jenny for Laurie's part?"

"Not exactly planned," Miss Polly answered. "But I do think it would be nice. I'm almost sure Mr. Harris thought so too. And it isn't as though Laurie would lose everything, is it? Besides, she's already made a place for herself in life, and she'll have other opportunities."

Reuben sighed. "I just hope if Jenny does get the part, I won't have to be the one to give Laurie the bad news."

Laurie spoke from the doorway. "You mean about me and the dulcimer?" She put down her breakfast tray. "Laurie *hates* playing the dulcimer, and Laurie thinks Jenny would be perfect for the part. Don't worry. It would be no bad news to me," she grinned.

"Don't tell Mr. Harris that," Reuben Kinkaid said. "You don't have to *give* him back his contract, you know."

"I'll leave the business details up to you, Mr. Kinkaid, per usual," Laurie replied airily.

At that moment the telephone rang. "I'll get it," Reuben Kinkaid said, pushing back his chair. "Probably Mr. Harris. And Laurie, don't talk about this in front of Tracy. Remember, Maribelle Jennings is her bosom friend. I'd at least like to get the facts straight before the news spreads."

By ten o'clock, Tracy was dropped off at the Jennings' cabin, Reuben was heading for a meeting with Mr. Harris, and Shirley and Chris were on their way to a Honeybee doctor to check Chris's foot, "just to be on the safe side," as his mother said.

Following the convertible into Honeybee was the blue pick-up truck with Keith at the wheel and Danny and Tom Sadd beside him.

"Too bad we couldn't have planned our ride in the cool of the morning," Tom said, looking out over the valley. "It's going to be hot down there by afternoon."

"Maybe we can fix it up for around five o'clock," Keith replied. "Say, listen Tom, this trip into Honeybee isn't exactly just to set up the horseback riding with Mr. MacFarlane. A couple of things have happened that we haven't had a chance to tell you. You know last night when Danny and I rushed off to pick up Jenny?"

Tom nodded.

"Well, that trip wasn't just for one reason either. Officer Clingley met us there. Danny and I each had something to tell the State troopers. He met us at the Jennings because it's better if Mom and the others don't know about it."

91

"Know about what?" Tom asked.

Briefly, Keith told his part of the story. "Now it's your turn, Danny, and just the facts, please."

Danny managed to be equally brief. "So you see, Tom," he ended admiringly, "Your hunch was right. And I didn't know what Keith saw, and he didn't know what I found. But I didn't want to tell you about it yesterday because of Chris."

"There hasn't been a chance to tell you until now," Keith added. "It wasn't that we wanted to leave you out of it. Man! The whole thing was your idea."

Tom shook his head. "I'm glad I didn't know," he sighed. "There goes my big chance of finding the money. The police will really move in now, and they'll be the ones to get the money."

Suddenly he sat up straight. "How come they aren't parked up at the lodge now? You'd think they'd have been out combing the area first thing this morning."

Keith shrugged. "Maybe they figure all they have to do is wait. He can't live in the mountains forever. Anyhow, we'll find out something when we see Officer Clingley. He's probably wondering why we're so late getting to see him."

"I'm wondering too," Danny said. "I'll bet Mr. Kinkaid's beat us into Honeybee by ten minutes, you've been poking along so."

"What are we seeing Clingley for?" Tom asked.

"We have to sign stuff about the evidence we gave him," Danny answered. "And there ought to be a lab report too."

"On what?" Tom asked.

"Whiskers, whiskers in the razor," Danny answered

promptly. "They'll have to match them up with somebody's, won't they?"

Much to Danny's disappointment, no report was ready and waiting on either the whiskers or the wig. And Keith was almost as disappointed to hear Officer Clingley say that the police believed the mysterious legs in the thicket probably belonged to an unsociable mountain man—someone who, for reasons of his own, didn't want to be seen.

"But wouldn't you people want to check out this kind of information?" Tom asked. "Maybe there'd be signs of a campfire, something to show that a man had been staying up there a few days."

Officer Clingley shook his head. "According to the FBI description, the guy on the plane left it with only one bundle—money. It isn't likely he jumped prepared to camp out."

Tom's jaw set stubbornly. "I've read about lots of survival cases in the wilderness. He could go around eating berries. And if he'd carried even a Boy Scout knife, he'd be able to cut branches for some sort of shelter."

"But Tom, wait a minute," Keith said. "You said yourself that you thought the skyjacker had hidden the money and would come back for it, maybe weeks later."

Tom shook his head. "That was before I heard about your seeing those legs. I just can't believe that somebody would hide in that undergrowth for a couple of hours just because he was 'unsociable.' If he didn't want to meet up with people, he'd just beat it, wouldn't he?"

Officer Clingley laughed. "I see you don't know mountain men, Tom. They do pretty much as the notion strikes them. Maybe he'd been having a try at finding the money himself, and was just curious about what you folks were doing." He paused. "I'll tell you the one thing that upsets the theory that the skyjacker is either lurking around up there or got away —it's that jacket we recovered. What sane man would throw away a jacket with a wallet that had seventy-three dollars in it? Nope! Sooner or later, a body is going to wash up below the gorge. Just you wait."

Tom stood up. "I guess nobody will mind if I keep on looking while I wait, will they?"

"Go ahead," Officer Clingley said. "Just don't do your searching too near the gorge. That river could pull you off your feet before you could say 'Tom Sadd'!"

"But what if Tom's right?" Danny asked, frowning. "What if that skyjacker is still there? It would be pretty dangerous for Tom, wouldn't it?"

Officer Clingley hesitated. "Tom will have to decide that for himself. But the police aren't going to give him an escort. It's up to him what he does."

But all the way to Mr. MacFarlane's brother's place, which was three miles on the other side of Honeybee, Danny worried.

"I just don't believe the police have given up on this, no matter what we heard back there."

"Why not?" Keith asked.

"Whiskers," Danny answered. "Why would they have sent in for a lab report on whiskers if downstream they expected to find . . . er, the jaw?"

" 'Routine, ma'am. Just routine,' " Keith grinned. "Now come on, Danny. Get your great brain going on how much it will cost to rent five horses for two hours."

"At how much per?"

"Only Mr. MacFarlane knows," Keith answered.

Danny sighed. "Man, you just don't *think*, Keith."

"No? What about?"

"Feeding the computer," Danny flashed back, grinning.

Chapter 10

□ By the time the "horse-party," as Danny called it, had gathered in Mr. MacFarlane's stableyard, the heat of the sun was gone from the day. The sky was blue and clear.

Mr. MacFarlane and his helpers had led out the horses from the old stable, and Courtney Cross and Tom Sadd had picked two palominos. Keith was mounted on a roan, and Laurie had chosen a satin black mare that Mr. MacFarlane called "Waltzing Matilda."

"She's notional," he warned. "Takes to dancing like a duck to water. But you just let her know who's boss, and she'll give you a good ride."

It was Jenny's choice that had everybody laughing, even Jenny. "I don't care," she giggled, as Mr. Mac-Farlane led out "Colonel," a tremendous dapple gray.

"Are you sure, Jenny?" Keith asked doubtfully. "He's so big he won't even know you're in the saddle. I thought you said you wanted a nice elderly little horse."

Mr. MacFarlane helped boost Jenny into the saddle. "Jenny knows what she's doing," he smiled. "Colonel's been around here a long time. And he's a real responsible fellow. Heck! You might almost say he has power steering and an automatic transmission, he's that easy, aren't you boy?" He patted Colonel's muzzle.

Jenny, who now towered over everybody else, stroked Colonel's neck. "Do you want us to start out on the meadow trail, Mr. MacFarlane?"

"Nope. Better take the uptrail while the horses are fresh. That way, you'll get a nice view from Lookout Point, and the horses won't be so tempted by that meadow grass when they're heading back for the barn."

The black mare was friskily side-stepping and jiggling her bridle. "I can see why you call her Waltzing Matilda," Laurie called over to the others. "I think she's asking me for the next dance. Can't we get started?"

"Let Colonel take the lead," Mr. MacFarlane said. "It would hurt his feelings not to be at the head of the regiment." He gave Colonel's dappled rump a slap. "I'll be looking for you before dark, now," he called after them.

The "uptrail," as Mr. MacFarlane called it, was a broad, pine-needled stretch that reached along for nearly a mile before it began climbing above the valley. Jenny, looking very small, walked Colonel along at a slow jog.

"Do you think Colonel's dignity would be insulted if we went on ahead?" Courtney Cross called out.

Jenny turned in the saddle. "Mine would be," she

called back, laughing. She swung Colonel into an easy canter.

But it wasn't long before the two palominos overtook Colonel. "Wait for me at the first fork," Jenny called after them, as Tom and Courtney loped on ahead.

Keith checked the roan and fell in beside Jenny. Behind them Laurie called, "I'm going to have a few words with Matilda, so watch out."

In a flash, Matilda's neat hoofs were kicking up sandy pine-needle puffs as she passed at a fast trot.

"Keith, you needn't stay back on my account," Jenny said. "Why don't you ride on ahead?"

"Oh, I don't mind," Keith grinned, his eyes about level with Jenny's ear. "I'm the type who likes to look up to women—about two feet up, I'd say."

Jenny looked down at the roan's bobbing head. "My guess is more like one foot," she replied, grinning. "I wish I could ride like Laurie. She's marvelous."

"Pretty good," Keith agreed. "Not so great on the dulcimer, though. Say, how does it feel to suddenly become a movie actress?"

Jenny flushed. "I'm no actress. When Mr. Harris called this morning, he said all I'd have to do is to sit on a log and sing. That's not exactly acting. I feel sort of silly about the whole thing."

"Don't," Keith advised. "Laurie's a winner. She likes to succeed. But really, she wasn't very crazy about this part. Now she can do a lot of riding, and you know you can't sit on a log and sit on a horse at the same time."

"I'm more the sit-on-a-log type," Jenny sighed.

"But anyhow, Laurie's been wonderful to me, and I *am* thrilled about this chance."

They jogged along silently. "Laurie likes Tom Sadd a lot, doesn't she?" Jenny asked suddenly.

"Oh, Laurie likes lots of people," Keith replied. "Sort of one after another. Why?"

Jenny hesitated. "Oh, I don't know, but Tom's so *odd*. One time he's a lot of fun, like at the square dance. Then other times, he looks as though he wishes he didn't even have to bother to say 'hello.'"

"I guess he has lots to worry about," Keith said. "I asked him what he's planning to do when we leave here, and he said he'd just keep on staying around here until he can get enough money together for a new bike. He said he'd like to pedal all the way down to Florida and do an article on the Florida Everglades for his magazine."

"That's pretty practical when you think about it," Jenny said thoughtfully. "I mean, being a writer he probably wants to really observe. And you can see more from a bike than an airplane."

"Mom wants to do something for him, and so do I," Keith said. "But it's hard to know how to go about it. We can't just *give* him a bike. He'd think we were sorry for him, and he'd sure hate that.—Hey! Look who's coming."

Around the curve in the trail ahead, the palomino with Tom in the saddle came loping into view.

"I think we're being called for," Jenny said.

Keith laughed. "They probably thought Colonel died of old age."

Tom pivoted the palomino, as Keith and Jenny trotted their horses. Tom grinned. "We began to

100

worry about you two—or you four, I should say. We thought Colonel got mad and went home."

Jenny laughed. "Colonel's just been wondering when this ride is going to start. Fall in, men!" With a *tch*, *tch*, and touching her heels to the dapple's flanks, Jenny was off in a cloud of dust.

Twilight was turning the sky rosy by the time Colonel led the others back into the stableyard.

"It was wonderful, Mr. MacFarlane!" Laurie exclaimed.

Mr. MacFarlane smiled. "Matilda give you a good ride, did she?"

"The best," Laurie smiled back. "If it's a nice day tomorrow, could we ride in the morning?"

"I can't," Keith said quickly. "I'm helping Tom tomorrow. We're rigging up an outdoor shower for Miss Polly."

"A shower!" Courtney Cross exclaimed. "How about my helping out? I'm a pretty good man with a plumber's wrench. My dad's a plumber, and he was going to take me into the business when this movie thing started."

"Welcome to the union," Tom grinned.

"We'll pick you up in Honeybee when we go down in the morning after the pipe and supplies Tom needs," Keith said.

Laurie sighed. "There go three men at once. How about you, Jenny?"

"Can't. Mr. Harris told me to report for work."

"That makes me the Lone Ranger, I guess." Laurie bent over and swatted at the knees of her jeans. "Oh! *Oh!*" she gasped.

101

"What's the matter!" everybody asked at once.

"My back!" Laurie gasped. "Something's happened. I can't straighten up. Oh!"

"There, there, now," Mr. MacFarlane said quietly. "Don't be scared. Happens to me all the time. I can heave a saddle up on a horse one day and put out my back lifting an egg the next. Just keep calm."

"I am calm," Laurie wailed. "I'm so calm I can't move."

"No need to." Mr. MacFarlane turned to Keith. "Why don't you just drive that pick-up right over here? We can put a padding of hay in the back and lift her up there nice as you please."

The ride back was miserable for Laurie even though she was lying on a deep nest of sweet smelling hay, and Tom was sitting beside her. Tears squeezed down her face. "Nothing—*nothing's* working out right for me," she thought miserably. "This is what I get for not really *trying* when Mr. Kinkaid got me that part. I'll probably never be able to even wiggle again. And I'll miss the Labor Day concert, and I'll just be forgotten by the whole world."

She sobbed aloud.

Shirley Partridge walked down the lodge steps with Dr. Kennedy. "You're sure Laurie doesn't belong in a hospital, Doctor?" she asked worriedly. "This seems so odd. Shouldn't she have x-rays? She's never been sick a day since she was eight years old, and then it was only mumps."

Dr. Kennedy smiled. "And mumps gave her more trouble than this will. She isn't sick, Mrs. Partridge, only miserable. This may last for a few days, or maybe only a few hours. These back things are mysterious. It's your son, Chris, you'll really have to keep an eye on for a day or so. See that he keeps that foot soaking. Don't worry now. I'll call tomorrow and check on both my patients."

No sooner had Dr. Kennedy's car started down the drive, than Mr. Harris drove up in a station wagon.

"Now what!" Shirley said to Reuben Kinkaid and Miss Polly. "I'm in no mood to discuss being a dead grandmother. What's needed around here is a very *live* mother."

Mr. Harris asked how Laurie and Chris were feeling and exchanged a few words with Miss Polly. "I really shouldn't have bothered you this evening," he said to Shirley. "But it seemed important enough to talk over as soon as possible. You see, we've been worried all along about one part of the script. And then this afternoon everything seemed to fall into place. We've decided the only thing to do is to switch around some of the scenes so that the role of the grandmother and granddaughter could be played by the same actress. By using Jenny in a double role we think—"

Shirley tilted her chair forward. "You mean I'm *fired?*" she interrupted.

"That isn't the word I intended to use," Mr. Harris said regretfully, "But, yes."

Shirley swung the rocker wildly back and burst out laughing. Reuben scowled and Mr. Harris looked puzzled. "Mr. Harris, you're the brightest spot in the entire day," she gasped. "The *very* brightest."

Reuben Kinkaid hastily spoke. "Shirley, I think

103

you are over-tired. Why don't you let me iron out details like a contract with Mr. Harris?"

"Iron out details!" Miss Polly exclaimed. "Looks to me like Mr. Harris has done all the ironing needed around here. This is the first time today Shirley's so much as had a smile on her face. And now look at her—happy as a little lark!"

Shirley burst into a fresh attack of giggles.

"More like happy as a little *nut*," Reuben Kinkaid said gruffly. "I've never seen movie careers come and go faster than yours and Laurie's."

"What's all the fun about?" Danny Partridge asked as he stepped out on the porch. Keith and Tom followed him.

"Your mother's just been fired," Reuben said gloomily.

"She *has!*" Danny exclaimed. "Oh Mom, that's great. Wait until I tell Chris! I bet his heel will get better right away." He dashed to the door. "I'll tell Laurie too," he said, turning back. "You can't tell, maybe this whole thing around here is psychosomatic. Psychosomatic is when you're sick but you're not sick with what you think you're sick about," he explained. "Back in a minute." He slammed the door and went racing off through the lobby.

Reuben Kinkaid chuckled. "As the Partridge Family business agent *I'm* sick. But at least I know what I'm sick about—six stick-together Partridges. Next time I try to help this family develop as individuals, somebody stop me, please."

"Well, there's always a chance of a Partridge Family movie," Mr. Harris said.

"There is?" Keith exclaimed.

"We'll talk about it before we leave," Mr. Harris promised. He turned to Miss Polly. "I heard about the scholarships you plan, Miss Polly, and I think maybe Frameway Films might like to add a little something to its payment to you. That's a fine plan you have."

Miss Polly beamed. "That would be very nice," she said. "And I imagine that now with Jenny doing twice as much as she was hired to do, she'll earn twice as much, won't she? That will be nice, too."

It was Mr. Harris's turn to burst out laughing. "I'm beginning to see where your nephew gets his business talents, Miss Polly."

"This occasion calls for lemonade," Miss Polly said rising. "Will you help me, Shirley?"

Mr. Harris leaned back comfortably and watched the stars come twinkling out in the darkening sky. "I must say that doing business with the Partridge Family is certainly pleasant. Now if we could only get Tom, here, fixed up with something, I'd say this part of the summer was a hundred percent success around here."

Tom creaked his rocker noisily. "Don't worry about me," he said gruffly. "I've sidetracked myself. I think I can interest my publisher in a book on the ecology of the Florida Everglades. So I'll be pushing on soon."

From the porch steps Danny exclaimed, "Aw, Tom! You're not going to leave right when we're just starting the rock collection, are you? We don't have to talk about what a wonderful family we are. It must be gruesome to listen to. But it only happens now and then. Don't leave."

Tom grinned. "I'd better help with the lemonade. Stick around here and who knows? I might have my head turned."

Just then, there was a tremendous spread of purple-red lightning across the sky. Danny leaped to his feet. "Hey! Are we going to have a storm?"

"It's just heat lightning," Reuben Kinkaid said. "But the long range weather forecast is stormy weather next week or later."

Mr. Harris sighed. "I hope it's later. We need a run of good weather for those outdoor shots."

Miss Polly chirped from the doorway. "Here we come! Coconut cake, anybody?"

Danny put down his cake plate. "You know, I just thought of something," he announced. "And it's good luck, I think."

"If it's good luck, let's hear it," Keith said.

"You remember how we had thirteen people twice at the table? And remember how each time the panther screamed?"

"That doesn't sound so lucky so far," Keith said, "But go ahead."

"Simple," Danny continued. "One time must have been for Chris's heel, and the next time it meant Laurie's back."

"That blows your psychosomatic theory," Reuben Kinkaid laughed.

Danny frowned. "Oh well, I have two ideas going. You can take your choice," he said airily.

As though in answer a sharp, blood-curdling screech sounded and quivered away to silence in the dark night.

Danny knocked over his glass and lemonade streamed down the steps. "Oh wow," he whispered shakily. "He's doing it now with just six of us."

"And this time, it must be your bad luck," Keith said lightly. "There's no more lemonade."

Everybody made some sort of remark—everybody but Tom Sadd. Still as stone, he stared out into the dark.

Chapter 11

☐ Whether or not Danny's idea was right that his mother's being at home was going to cure Chris and Laurie, each was much better in the morning. The angry spreading red was nearly gone from Chris's foot, and Laurie was at least able to move carefully to a pillow-padded rocker on the porch.

Tom and Chris sat at a card table working on an assortment of small rocks—making out labels, rubbing the white tiles to get color streaks from the rocks, and jotting down information in their notebooks.

"We've got some nice garnets here," Tom said.

"Garnets? Which ones are garnets?" Danny asked. "That's my birthstone—January. What month were you born, Tom?"

"August," Tom replied.

"August what?" Chris asked.

Tom laughed. "I don't know. Neither does anybody else."

"You mean you were left on somebody's door-step?" Chris asked wide-eyed.

"I didn't get even that far," Tom replied. "I got left in a park—me and an ice cream cone. And that melted. I can remember that much."

"Then what happened?" Danny asked eagerly.

"Nothing much," Tom answered.

"Aw, come on Tom. Tell us," the boys pleaded.

"I went for a hike, along with my bike, because that's what I like," Tom sing-songed. "Come on, you guys, if you want to get these rocks recorded with any help from me."

"Hey, Tom," Keith called from the doorway. "Got a peridot there?"

"Yes. Why?"

"That's your birthstone. I just looked up August in the almanac."

"Eavesdropper!" Tom grinned.

Keith stepped out on the porch. "Who's doing what today?"

"I'm going to soak my foot," Chris said disgustedly. "Maybe I'll write out my annual report and get that much out of the way for school."

"What's your annual report?" Keith asked.

Chris sighed. "This year it will be called, 'How I Spent My Vacation in Miss Polly's Dishpan.' "

Laurie giggled. "I'll be around to keep you company, Chris."

Danny looked up. "I'd be free for any interesting activity. What do you have in mind?"

"Groceries," Keith replied. "Mrs. Griggs has quite a list."

Danny scrunched down in his chair. "Thanks, but no." He yawned.

"Okay, Mom and I will have to manage without your great advice on the best buys," Keith replied.

"Stay away from veal and the better cuts of beef," Danny flashed back, "and I'm sure you'll get along okay."

Keith thumped the almanac lightly on his brother's red head. "Consider yourself brained," he said pleasantly.

Shirley Partridge looked across the valley as Keith slowed the pick-up at Hairpin Bend. "I wish we could do something for Tom," she sighed. "He's such a loner, though. You never know when he's going to stand back and give you an icy stare or when he's going to be lots of fun."

Keith nodded. "That's what Jenny said. He doesn't say too much. I just found out his birthday's this month."

"When?"

"He doesn't know. I guess being an orphan sort of leaves its mark on a kid. Not to know you ever belonged anywhere, or worse, finding out you never belonged anywhere."

Shirley nodded. "Do you think we could just make up a birthday for him?" she asked. "We could have a party. Keith, why not? It would be a wonderful excuse for getting him a bicycle and a new backpack."

"I don't know. Tom can be awfully odd acting sometimes, and when you least expect it." He thought a minute. "You know, I was thinking about his birthstone. It's a peridot. Do you think we could get him a ring, or something?"

Shirley laughed. "You were wondering how he'd feel about a party and a bicycle just one second ago. Now it's a ring. I don't think so, Keith."

"Well, let's take a chance on a bicycle. We could ask at the Honeybee Hardware about one, and about a backpack, too."

To the Partridge's pleasure, Honeybee Hardware was able to get a bike and camping gear sent out from Asheville no later than Saturday.

"But I'm not for a big party," Shirley said, still thinking about Tom as they piled grocery sacks into the back of the pick-up. "I don't think Tom would like that. But let's have a 'Sunday-dinner-family-only' kind of party. What do you say?"

When they came back to Chestnut Lodge, they found that Tom and Danny had gone swimming, so it was the ideal time to discuss plans for Sunday.

Mrs. Griggs said, "I'll contribute the cake, chocolate, with writing on it. Something like, 'We're glad to know Tom Sadd.' How's that?"

Everybody agreed no greeting could be better.

Miss Polly thought a minute. "I have your Uncle Arthur's tie stickpin, Reuben. It's a fine gem peridot. He found it himself right here on the place and had it made up at the Honeybee Jewelers. Would you mind if I made it my gift to Tom? It's his birthstone, you know."

Reuben hastily looked away. "I don't think

they've been wearing stickpins lately, Aunt Polly."

"I know *that!*" Miss Polly said impatiently. "But it's the thought that counts, or so I was brought up to believe. But you could give him a check to have it reset into a ring, that is, if he fancies rings."

"Here come Tom and Danny now," Shirley said. "Goodness, that was a short swim. Now Tracy, not a word about the party, remember."

They heard the outdoor shower gushing and sputtering, then Tom came around the side of the lodge, a towel slung around his shoulders. With hardly a word to anyone, he came up the porch steps and went slamming into the lodge.

"Something's wrong," Shirley murmured.

Danny was next up the steps. "Have a good swim?" Keith asked. Danny nodded and marched to the door.

"Danny," Shirley called. "Wait a minute."

Danny stopped. "What?"

"Did you and Tom quarrel?" Shirley asked quietly. Danny shook his head.

"What's wrong, then?"

Danny shuffled uneasily from foot to foot. "Aw, it's just Tom," he burst out. "We hardly got there when he said we had to come back. He thinks someone's tailing him."

"Tailing him!" Aunt Polly exclaimed. "Why would anybody do such a thing? And how, for that matter?"

"Danny means Tom thinks someone is following him," Keith said.

"He says he's seen the bushes move before," Danny said. "But this time he heard branches snap and somebody running."

"Did you hear it too?" Keith asked.

Danny nodded. "Probably just some old bear."

"Bear!" Shirley gasped. "Don't tell me there are bears around here!"

"Certainly," Miss Polly said. "My generation didn't exterminate *everything*, you know."

"Well, Tom showed his usual good sense," Shirley said. "Don't you think so, Keith?"

Keith strolled over to the door. "Sure," he answered, almost absent-mindedly. "Why not?"

The door slammed behind him.

Keith knocked at Tom's door. "Hey, it's me."

Tom flung open the door. "Yes?"

"Danny says you think you're being tailed," Keith said. "Is that right?"

Tom stepped back. "Come on in," he said shortly.

Keith sat down on the foot of Tom's bed. "What's up?"

Tom belted his jeans. "Keith, did you ever get the feeling you're wading through molasses?"

Keith stared. "How do you mean?"

"Well, I have it," Tom replied. "I keep telling myself that money is around here somewhere, just waiting for me. And all the time, I've got this weird feeling that I'll *find* the money, but I'm never going to leave." He flung himself down on the bed and stared up at the ceiling.

Keith looked puzzled. "But what has that to do with the idea someone's following you?"

"It isn't an idea," Tom replied. "Somebody or some *thing* is. I feel it all the time."

Keith hesitated. "It doesn't sound like such a big

problem to me, Tom. Why don't we go to the police again? If that guy I saw is still poking around, then he's a lunatic. Let's get Officer Clingley on this."

Tom shook his head. "He'd say *I* was the lunatic." He jumped to his feet, walked over to the window, and stared out at the blue mountains. Suddenly he turned around and smiled. "Keith, do me a favor, will you?"

"Sure."

"Let me worry about this. Okay?"

"I guess I'll have to," Keith answered. "But in case you change your mind, count on me."

Tom turned away from the window and his face lighted with a smile. "Thanks. Thanks a lot."

In spite of Keith's worries, the Sunday "family party" couldn't have been a greater success. Before dessert, Tracy pushed back her chair.

"This is a party and I wrote a poem. It's for Tom."

Before Tom could even look surprised, Tracy was reading:

> Dear Tom Sadd,
> Don't get mad
> This is a birthday party for you
> And it will have to do.
> Love from me and everybody,
> Tracy Partridge.

Pink-faced, she sat down.

Mrs. Griggs came sailing in from the kitchen with her promised cake. She set it before Tom. He rose to his feet and read the greeting aloud. "Mrs. Griggs, this is a *real* first! Thanks a lot!"

Next came Aunt Polly's present, the stick pin, and Reuben's check.

"Now we adjourn to the porch soon as you cut the cake," Danny said. "Our present's out there."

Cake plates in hand, everybody trooped out to the big verandah.

"There she is," Chris said proudly. He waved his arm toward the shining green and silver bicycle propped on its standard at the foot of the steps. Strapped on the carrier was a neatly folded backpack.

"Say!" Tom exclaimed. "Say! What is this!"

"Try it out," Tracy squealed.

A strange look came over Tom's face. Slowly, he walked down the steps. He patted the backpack, put his hand on the handlebars, and looked back at the crowd on the front steps. "You shouldn't have, as they say. But thanks."

"Try her out," Chris urged.

Tom hesitated, then swung one leg over the crossbar.

"You better put up the kick-stand first," Danny called out.

Tom looked up toward the verandah. He swung his leg back. "You know folks, I don't want to ride it one inch—not until the day I go."

He walked back up the steps. "I think I'll just sit here and look at it," he said. "Sure is a beauty."

"Don't look too long," Miss Polly said. "See that sky over in the west? We'll have rain before evening or I miss my guess."

Chapter 12

□ By Tuesday morning life was back to normal at Chestnut Lodge. Laurie was much better, and Chris's foot was so improved that the dishpan was returned to its nail on the cellar staircase wall—forever, he hoped.

"Now that his family is back in shape," Reuben said after breakfast, "I'm flying up to New York."

"Whatever for?" Miss Polly asked.

"Because I don't like to hear endless hours of rock music—in practice form, that is," Reuben grinned.

"Aw, Mr. Kinkaid!" Chris and Danny said together. "It's still our vacation!"

"Labor Day and the concert will be here before you know it," Reuben replied. "And now that your mother and sister have given up careers in the movies, this family had better shape up as the outstanding rock group they're supposed to be. Money doesn't grow on trees, you know. Okay, Shirley?"

"Okay," she smiled. "That seems fair. When will you be back?"

"Saturday morning, or maybe Friday night. Then we'll all be leaving here Sunday. I'll drive to the airport so you needn't worry about meeting planes. By the way, I forgot to tell you—everybody's invited by Mr. Harris to have dinner with him at the Honeybee Hotel on Saturday night."

"Is Maribelle invited?" Tracy asked.

"Now how could Mr. Harris have a party without Maribelle?" Reuben asked. "He wouldn't think of it."

"Why don't we all drive into the airport and see you off?" Shirley suggested. "Keith could bring us back in the pick-up. I have a few things I'd like to shop for in the city, and maybe the kids could find a movie they'd like to see."

Reuben laughed. "The perfect way to get ready for your concert—and after that great lecture I gave, too."

Shirley laughed and stood up. "We'd better start getting ready."

"Oh, I'm not leaving until tomorrow," Reuben said. "Didn't I say that? Tom and I are picking up some roofing materials this morning. He's going to patch up that leak on the porch roof. One more rain like the one Sunday night and the old roof has had it. Then this afternoon I have to see Mr. Harris on business."

"Our new picture?" Danny asked.

"Your mother's and sister's *old* picture," Reuben growled. "*Contract* details, as Laurie calls it."

After Reuben Kinkaid and Tom, with Chris tucked between them, drove off, Keith, Tracy, and Danny started off for Miss Polly's "swimming hole."

As Tracy trotted on ahead, Danny was unusually quiet.

"What's on your mind?" Keith asked.

Danny shook his head. "Not much."

"Come on, Danny," Keith grinned. "What's the great brain working on now?"

Danny stopped walking. He looked up at Keith. "Tom," he answered quietly.

"Oh, you don't have to worry about Tom, Danny. He's just a fellow who likes to go his own way. He wouldn't like to hang around with us forever."

"That's not exactly what I'm worrying about," Danny said slowly.

"Then what's the problem?"

Danny bent down and pulled up a long grass blade. "I don't think Tom knows how to ride a bike," he said evenly, not looking at Keith.

"You don't think that Tom can—" Keith exploded into laughter. "Someone who's always telling everybody to put two and two together ought to know that two and two make four. You're coming up five, or something."

"How?" Danny asked, unblinkingly.

"Tom was *on* a bike when he came up here."

Danny shook his head. "He was walking."

"You know what I mean," Keith said impatiently. "You know why he was walking. Man! That was the start of all his troubles."

Danny sighed. "Okay, I guess you're right." He began to walk ahead.

119

"Wait a minute," Keith said. "What got you started on this idea, anyhow?" He fell into step beside Danny.

"Just what I said. I thought it was funny not to try out a great new bike like that."

Keith shook his head. "Tom was just embarrassed —the birthday party, all that fuss made over him— then getting the bike. I'd feel the same way."

"It wouldn't embarrass me," Danny said.

"I can believe it," Keith grinned.

Tracy came walking back toward them. "I've waited and waited," she called out crossly. "Aren't we ever going swimming? It's getting cloudy. Maybe it'll rain before we even get there."

"Bet you it won't," Keith smiled. And he was half-right—the rain held off. It was nighttime before it came, and then it was a downpour.

"Good morning, good morning," Miss Polly sang out as Shirley came into the kitchen. "Did you ever see a prettier day in your life?"

"Never did," Shirley agreed. "That storm last night really cleared the air. But what are you doing getting breakfast? Where's Mrs. Griggs?"

"Not coming," Miss Polly answered, tapping an eggshell. "But I haven't forgotten how to scramble eggs and fry bacon."

"Neither have I. Let me help. Is Mrs. Griggs ill?"

"She'd say, worse than that," Miss Polly replied. "Their roof leaked, and straight into the closet where she keeps the bedding. She says she had to hang nearly every quilt and blanket she owns out on the clothesline, and you know what a chore that would be. I told her not to bother with us. If you folks are back in time for dinner, we'll just take potluck, don't you think?"

"Why not," Shirley answered. "But Laurie will be here to help. She's decided to pamper her back and stay home. And I'm glad she's showing such good sense."

Miss Polly smiled. "I imagine Tom will be glad too. Maybe he and Laurie would like to take a picnic lunch down by the swimming hole if she feels up to it. That boy certainly earned his salt with all the work he did on the porch roof yesterday. I think he should have the day off."

Danny strolled into the kitchen. "Who's having a picnic?"

"Tom and Laurie—maybe. Laurie's decided to stay home today."

"That's funny," Danny said. "I've decided on that, too."

Shirley looked over at her redheaded son. "Well, it seems as though the party's getting smaller. What's changed your mind?"

Danny opened a cupboard door and lifted down a cereal bowl. "I have some work I'd like to get out of the way. Could I use your portable typewriter, Mom?"

Shirley nearly dropped the melon slice she was putting on a plate. "Getting *work* out of the way! Danny, are you sure this isn't a hasty decision? You'll be missing a movie, you know."

Danny shook his head. "Nope. First things first, I always say."

"If that's what you always say, then I'd better have

my hearing checked," his mother said. "But okay. The portable's on the desk in my room. Paper too. Help yourself."

At the last minute, it was decided to leave the pick-up behind. There was plenty of room in Reuben Kinkaid's car now that two Partridges were staying behind, and Keith would call for Reuben on Saturday morning.

"The keys are in the pick-up," Keith called back as they began to roll along the driveway.

Tom waved and shook his head. He turned to Laurie. "I never did get that temporary driver's permit," he said.

"It doesn't matter," Laurie replied. "We wouldn't be driving to the swimming hole, anyhow."

Danny clapped a hand to his forehead. "The swimming hole isn't exactly the only place on earth, you know," he said, adding a large groan to his words. "A driver's license is a very useful thing."

Laurie flipped her long hair back. "If my conversation is *too* painful, you poor, dear soul, I can only suggest that you disappear to another part of the world. In fact, didn't you tell Mom you had some work to get out of the way?"

Danny grinned. "I believe I did. Maybe I ought to get at it so I'll be free to join you and Tom at your pool-side picnic."

He hopped rapidly past Laurie and hurried through the doorway. "See you later, you poor, dear soul," he called back cheerfully through the screening.

In less than five minutes he was back at the door. "Laurie, Mom said I could use her portable. But I can't get the roller to move. It goes around all right, but it won't go sideways. Is there something you press somewhere?"

"Tom," Laurie said. "Would you mind taking a look? You're the writer around here. I don't know much about typewriters."

Tom looked down at the little portable on Shirley's desk.

Danny struck at a key. "See. It hits all right but the roller doesn't move to the left for the next letter you hit."

"Hmm." Tom pushed the roller to the left. It didn't budge. "I guess something's stuck."

"I don't think that will help," Danny said, doubtfully. "Isn't there something that's catching it?"

Tom scowled. "Mine's a different model." He turned away. "Sorry, Danny, but I don't want to fool around with it and break something."

"Well, I'll experiment. The Partridge Family Rock Company won't ever get off the ground if we don't send out some letters." He flipped a small lever at the side of the keyboard, then struck a key. The roller moved to the left. "Hey! I've fixed it!" he exclaimed.

"Congratulations," Tom said. "I guess you're still in business. Want the door closed?"

Danny nodded. "Thanks."

Ten minutes later, Danny Partridge was still staring at the two words he had typed: Dear Sir. Slowly, he rolled the paper out of the machine, put it aside and rolled in a fresh sheet. It was lunchtime before he finished his typing, and he still hadn't finished even one business letter for the Partridge Family Rock Company.

Miss Polly looked across the table at Danny's plate. "You don't seem to have much of an appetite, Danny. Or don't you like ham sandwiches?"

"Oh, sure," Danny replied. "I guess I'm just not very hungry right now. Maybe I'll put it in the refrigerator and have it later."

Miss Polly put down her teacup. "Now I declare! I knew there was something I meant to ask Tom to do this morning, and it went right out of my mind when the idea of a picnic came in."

"What was it?" Danny asked politely. "Could I do it for you?"

Miss Polly thought a minute. "I don't know why not," she replied. "Mrs. Griggs' leaking roof set me to thinking about this one. I was going to ask Tom to take a look around in the attic to see if everything was dry. But if you'd take charge of the flashlight, I don't know why we couldn't find out for ourselves."

"Sure," Danny replied. "Anytime."

Miss Polly arose from her chair. "Let's do it right now before the notion strikes me to take a nap. I'll get the flashlight."

To Danny's surprise, the attic wasn't one big space. Doors along an entire side divided one half of it into storage rooms. There was enough daylight from the small dusty windows at either end so that the flashlight wasn't needed for seeing the way.

"What we have to do is shine the light on the floorboards," Miss Polly said. "If we see a wet spot, then we'll know there's a leak in the roof above." She followed behind Danny, and they walked over every part of the one big room.

"Dry as a bone!" she exclaimed. "And I must say I'm surprised. Now for the storage rooms, and we're through up here. Let's start at the far end and work our way back."

It was when they opened the door of the middle room that their search came to a sudden end. Water covered one entire corner, and no flashlight was needed to see why. Blue sky shone above a gap in the roof big enough for Tracy to have climbed through. Miss Polly stared up in astonishment, too amazed for speech.

"Oh, wow!" Danny exclaimed. "You wouldn't exactly call that a leak in the roof, would you?"

"It's more of a *hole*," Miss Polly answered faintly. "Now how on earth?"

Danny's glance went to the floor, and for once he was too startled to speak. Square in the middle of splintered shingles and blobs of rotted tar paper was a dark water-soaked bundle. And letters, only a shade darker than the canvas they were stenciled on, spelled out TRANS-EAST AIRLINES.

"Miss Polly," Danny whispered. "Look!" He stepped forward.

"You'll get your shoes wet," Miss Polly said. "Whatever it is, the damage is done. Don't bother with it, Danny. We'll get Tom to . . ."

Danny dragged at one strap of the dripping oblong and picked it up in both hands. Water streamed from

125

it, and water on the floor circled in a small rippling wave toward Miss Polly. She stepped back hastily. "What is it?" she asked nervously.

"The airlines money," Danny answered in an awe-struck voice. "It's been right here in your attic all the time!" He held the bundle out toward her.

Miss Polly stared. "And all along I thought it was a big cat landing on the roof! I heard it come through the roof and didn't know it!"

By the time Danny had helped Miss Polly down the steep attic stairs and then on down to the first floor, she was trembling with excitement. But she was her practical self again. "To the kitchen sink with it," she commanded. "I shall follow at my own pace."

Danny dashed on ahead, flinging recycled raindrops in all directions. He'd no sooner plopped the soggy canvas into the sink than he heard Miss Polly's voice.

"You'll never believe it—never. Follow me!"

His heart leaped to his throat as he heard Tom Sadd speak. "Never believe what, Miss Polly?"

Chapter 13

☐ "Now isn't that a sight for you?" Miss Polly asked. "Open it up, Danny. I've never yet seen three-hundred thousand dollars, and I mean to have a peek this minute!"

Danny tugged at the sodden straps and metal buckles.

"Here, I'll do it," Tom said roughly. He shoved Danny so hard that he stumbled and would have fallen if Laurie hadn't caught his shoulders.

Quickly he worked the straps free. "There you are Miss Polly," he said, laying back the wet flaps. "While you're taking your peek, I'd better call the police." He hurried out of the kitchen.

Danny stared after him, scowling.

"I don't think he meant to push you so hard, Danny," Laurie said softly. "He was just excited. Don't get mad."

Danny's eyes flickered. "I'm not mad," he answered. "I've just found out I was wrong about something. Man! Was I wrong! I've never been *wronger!*"

Slowly he walked out of the kitchen and into the lobby.

"That's all right," he heard Tom say. "Will you people notify the airlines or should Miss Kinkaid do it?" There was a short pause. Then Tom said, "Okay, then. We'll see you in a couple of hours."

Tom put down the phone and looked at Danny. "My hunch was right, wasn't it?" he grinned. "At least, it wasn't more than a mile off as the crow flies —or Trans-East Airlines flies."

"Why aren't the police coming right away?"

"If you can believe it, Officer Clingley's cruiser is in MacFarlane's garage for repairs. It won't be ready for an hour or so."

"That's funny," Danny frowned. "You'd think the State police would send out some other troopers then for something important as this."

Tom stood up. "Well, I might as well get packed up," he said.

"Packed up!" Danny exclaimed. "Why? You mean you're leaving?"

"Sure. The money's found—no reason to stick around this dump now."

Danny flushed an angry scarlet. "I guess it's such a dump that you won't even stop long enough to get your money from Miss Polly."

Tom took one step toward Danny, eyes flashing. Then he stopped and suddenly smiled. "Sure I'll get my money from Miss Polly. Why not?"

And turning on his heel he strode off to his room.

Danny sank down into the chair by the telephone and stared after Tom.

"If I had Tom figured right, he wouldn't have called the police," he told himself. "And maybe when he called this place a 'dump,' it was because he was so disappointed that he wasn't the one to find the money. Maybe I shouldn't have said what I said. But why would he pack up and go *now?* Everybody's leaving on Sunday. Why wouldn't he wait at least until then? Why should finding the money make such a big difference? I wish I could figure this out." He sighed, and swung his legs over the chair arm.

And suddenly Danny Partridge had the answer—it was dangling across his ankles. Tom Sadd had never called the police—he had cut the telephone line.

After his first shocked glance, Danny swung into action. He pushed the line back out of sight. "That's what he meant when he said, 'sure I'll get my money,'" Danny thought as he jumped up and ran for the kitchen. "*He's going to take the airlines money!*"

Miss Polly was just pouring a cup of tea for herself, and Laurie was opening a coke when Danny skidded through the doorway.

"We're standing guard on the—Danny! What's the matter?" Laurie cried.

Danny rushed to the sink and looked at the sodden stacks of bills. He whirled around and dashed to the refrigerator, then tore back to the sink.

"Danny, what's wrong with you?" Laurie asked in real alarm.

"Help—and don't ask questions," he gasped.

"Tom's going to come in here, and he's going to steal the money. Believe me, *please*. Here—" he held out two packs of bills to Laurie. "Put 'em in the freezer. *Hurry*."

Laurie didn't budge. Almost as though hypnotized, she and Miss Polly watched as Danny raced across the kitchen and wedged the packs into the freezer, then raced back to the sink for more until the canvas sack was emptied. With trembling fingers, he frantically began pulling frozen food packages from the freezer and piled them in the canvas sack. Then he folded down the wet flaps and buckled the straps into place.

It was only then that Danny Partridge realized he had made a fatal mistake. Tom Sadd would never be fooled by the weight and feel of the repacked bag.

"Have you lost your mind, Danny Partridge?" Laurie gasped. "What do you think you're doing?"

Before Danny could say a word, Tom Sadd came into the kitchen and strode to the sink. For a moment, he stared down at the strapped up canvas. Then, reaching out his fingers he pinched down on the edges of the packages beneath. They showed up in stiff outlines beneath his hand.

He turned swiftly to Danny. "Okay, smart kid." He lifted his hand and swooped it across Danny's face. "Where's the money? *Where?*"

"Tom!" Laurie cried. "Tom!"

Miss Polly got to her feet. "Thomas Sadd," she said sternly. "You're not to be more foolish than you already have been. First you throw away a bicycle, then you get ready to throw away your good name. I'll not let you be a common thief."

Tom laughed a short, ugly laugh. "*Common* thief?

I'm no *common* thief. Who do you think got this money in the first place. It's *mine*."

Miss Polly stepped square in front of him. "This is *not* your money. It belongs to the airlines. I won't let you do this."

"Try and stop me," Tom sneered. "Now where's the money?" He spread out his hand and pushed her with such force that she fell backward, lost her balance and crashed to the floor, striking her silvery head against the leg of the kitchen table. She lay very still, eyes closed.

Laurie screamed. She pushed past Tom and dropped to her knees beside Miss Polly. "You've killed her!" she cried out, voice trembling.

Tom jerked her to her feet. "Where's that money?" he asked in a slow, deadly voice.

"You won't find out from me—you, you *nothing!*" Laurie tried to twist out of his grasp.

Tom's eyes glittered. His hand balled into a knuckly fist. "No?" he asked. He drew back his arm.

Danny, white-faced, flung himself in front of Laurie. "You'll have to hit me first!" he shouted.

Miss Polly's blue eyes fluttered open. "Nobody's going to hit anybody," she said faintly. "Danny, give Tom the key to the barn door padlock." She pointed weakly to the kitchen table drawer above her head. "Laurie, help me get up."

Danny stared down at Miss Polly. The blow on her head must have affected her mind, he thought.

"Get it, Danny!" Miss Polly ordered. Her eyes closed again. Danny didn't move.

But Tom stepped to the table and jerked the drawer open. He picked up the big, old-fashioned key and stared down at Miss Polly. "It's my money," he repeated. "Mine." He glared at all three, then suddenly swung around and slammed out the back door.

Almost before he had started down the back steps, Miss Polly whispered, "Hurry. Help me to my feet. We'll lock ourselves in my room. We can holler through the door where the money is, and only pray he'll take it and go. *Tom Sadd is insane!*"

Danny's thoughts were churning. "It's all my fault this happened. What did I think Tom would do, anyhow? If he was mad in the kitchen, he'll be a raving maniac when all he finds in that barn is a terrible smell. And Miss Polly's room doesn't sound like any great protection to me. *If we could only get out of here.*"

And suddenly, like the click of a light switch, Danny Partridge had an idea. "Laurie, get a good hold on Miss Polly's arm. We're leaving—in the pick-up. *Run!*"

Miss Polly's small shoes hardly touched the floor as Laurie and Danny broke into a jolting trot to the front door, across the porch, and down the steps. Suddenly, Miss Polly sagged between them.

"She's fainted!" Laurie gasped.

"Then we'll have to get her in the back of the truck," Danny panted.

Together they lifted and heaved and hauled, until the small figure was lying on Mr. MacFarlane's hay nest. "You'd better ride beside her, Danny," Laurie said, "I'll drive." She started to get to her feet.

"Oh, Oh!"

"What's wrong?" Danny asked anxiously.

"I can't move! It's my back again. Danny, you'll have to drive."

"*Me?*" Even in his excitement, Danny froze to a standstill.

"You," Laurie said. "Danny, hurry! You know all the gadgets, and you can steer can't you? Hurry!"

Danny leaped down from the truck, stopping only long enough to fasten the tailgate, before hurrying on to the seat behind the wheel. He pushed on the starter, and the engine leaped to life. "There's only one thing—" he thought desperately. "I can hardly see over the wheel!"

Jerkily, he stepped on the gas and the bright blue pick-up leaped along the drive.

Whatever Danny's doubts were, they didn't compare with Laurie's. As they approached the steep turn at Hairpin Bend, Laurie forgot all about her back. Her heart pounded as Danny skirted dangerously close to the cable fencing. She squeezed her eyes shut. "Steering a bicycle and steering a car are two different things," she thought frantically.

When she dared to open her eyes again, the pick-up had come to a stop. They were smack in front of a no-parking sign, and smack in front of the Honeybee police station.

Chapter 14

☐ It was dark by the time Shirley and Keith rounded Hairpin Bend and glimpsed the lights of Chestnut Lodge in the distance. Chris and Tracy, sound asleep on the back seat, didn't awaken as Keith, a few minutes later, slowed the car and turned into the lodge drive.

"Hey, what's up? Officer Clingley must be calling on Miss Polly again," Keith said.

No Danny dashed down the steps to greet them, and the porch was shadowy and still.

Hurriedly, Shirley opened the car door. "I've a dreadful feeling something's wrong," she said. "I've had it ever since we tried to call her and learned the phone was out of order. Let's not wake the children, Keith. Come on."

Officers Clingley and Smith with Laurie and Danny were seated at the dining room table, papers spread out before them. The troopers got to their feet as Shirley Partridge and Keith came into the room.

Laurie, her face pale, looked up at her mother. Danny didn't smile. "Hi," he said quietly.

"What's happened? Where's Miss Polly? Laurie, what's wrong?" Shirley asked anxiously.

Officer Clingley answered for Laurie. "Everything's all right, ma'am," he said. "Miss Polly's okay. She's just spending the night in the Honeybee Clinic. But she's right as rain."

He pulled out a chair for Shirley. "We may as well start from the beginning, so's not to mix you up. Danny you'd better begin where you and Miss Polly were going up to the attic."

Shirley and Keith listened horror-struck as the story unfolded.

"And then," Laurie said, picking up the story where Danny left off, "We stayed right there at the Honeybee Clinic until visiting hours were over. And . . . and . . ." she suddenly raised her hands to her face, head bent.

Keith looked away from her and across to Officer Clingley. "I guess you have a warrant out for Tom's arrest, then?"

"We'll get to that in a few minutes," Officer Clingley said gruffly. "First, I'd like to read to you the report Danny gave us. He said he typed it out just this morning."

He picked up the sheets and began:

Report by Danny Partridge

1. Tom Sadd came to Chestnut Lodge walking. He said he'd lost his bicycle and his jacket.
2. He was worried most about losing his wal-

let. He said that meant he'd have to write for a new Social Security card and a new driver's license.

3. He never wrote any letters, and he never got any mail here.

4. His whiskers are dark. So was the wig I found.

5. When the police said they weren't going to search for the money, he said he thought it was still there and asked if they would mind if he kept looking for it. They said 'no'. But then he's never looked for it once after that. Maybe all the time he was really looking for the wig and razor I found, and the money-stuff was a big put-on.

6. If he'd hidden the money, he'd know where to find it. He didn't know. So I think his hunch wasn't a hunch at all. I think he only knew the money must be somewhere because *he was the one who dropped it.*

7. Maybe he stopped looking for the money because he thinks someone is watching him. I think so too—the police. I think that's why the police said the legs Keith saw weren't important. *They belonged to a policeman.* Maybe the police think he'll lead them to the money.

8. I don't think he knows how to ride a bike and that's why he wouldn't try his new bike.

9. I don't think he can type. Wouldn't a real writer know how to type? But he just stared at Mom's portable and didn't even try to fix it so the roller would move.

10. He's funny-acting about the panther. He

137

said it is a real loner. The man on the radio said Elmer Tell was a loner. Maybe Tom knows about loners because Tom Sadd is Elmer Tell.

Questions: Why didn't we ever hear about the lab report on the whiskers in the razor? Why didn't the police find out where Tom bought the travelers checks? Maybe he bought them in Buffalo.

(signed)
Danny Partridge.

Officer Clingley put down the papers. "Danny had everything pegged just about right. We wondered a lot about Tom Sadd right from the start. But his description didn't match up with Tell's, and it didn't seem likely that a skyjacker would be carrying travelers checks. But we ran a tracer on one he'd cashed at the Honeybee Department Store. Meantime, we deputized one of our mountain neighbors to keep an eye on anywhere Tom Sadd went around here. Danny was right. It was our man hiding that Keith saw. The report from the lab didn't mean too much excepting it showed the razor had shaved a dark beard. And the travelers checks were bought in New York City." He sighed. "Well, that's about it. We really didn't have anything on Tom Sadd."

"But what's happened since?" Keith asked. "Have you pulled him in, or what?"

"Tom's dead, Keith," Danny said in a low voice. "Dead!"

"We found him," Officer Clingley spoke. "When we came up here, the barn door was swinging wide. We won't ever know just how it all happened. Maybe he was kicking things around there in the half-dark. Maybe he had the cat cornered and didn't know it—but anyhow, that was the end of Elmer Tell."

"The *cat!*" Shirley exclaimed.

"Yes, ma'am. He was killed by the panther," Officer Clingley replied.

There was a long, long stillness.

Then Keith spoke. "I guess you've notified the air-lines."

"Oh, yes. First thing," Officer Clingley said. An odd expression came over his face. He looked at his fellow officer. "Did anybody take the money back down to headquarters?"

Officer Smith blushed. "Now that you mention it, no. I reckon it needs defrosting."

Miss Polly was ready and waiting to leave the Clinic when Danny knocked at her door in the morning. She beamed at him. "I don't have so much as a hat and purse to bother with. I'm all ready to go."

"Could we wait a minute, first?" Danny asked. "I have to tell you something."

"What's happened?" Miss Polly asked, looking at his serious face. "Didn't they catch Tom?"

"Tom's dead," Danny answered. He swallowed hard. "The panther was in the barn after all."

Miss Polly turned paper-white. She dropped into a chair and lifted her hands to her face. "I guess I might as well have murdered him as sent him out there," she said faintly. "I never *dreamed* it was still there."

"Of course you didn't know," Danny answered miserably. "We all know that, Miss Polly. You'd never meant things to turn out like they did."

Miss Polly closed her eyes. "I was just trying to give us time to get out of his way," she said tremblingly. She shook her head. "No, I didn't know," she said slowly. "No more than I knew years ago that the rock by the gorge was going to split away and carry old friends to their deaths."

She was silent for a moment. Then her eyes opened and she stood up. "I'd like to go home," she said shakily.

That evening Mr. Harris telephoned Miss Polly, and everybody at Chestnut Lodge who heard her end of the conversation noticed how much calmer the old lady had become.

"Call off your dinner party? Oh, I'd be most disappointed, Mr. Harris. I think that under the circumstances it would be better not to call it a party, though. Couldn't we just think of it as coming over for dinner? You see, I've been giving that evening a great deal of thought, and if I may, I'd like to give a short speech after the dessert."

Now it was Saturday night, and after the strawberry shortcake everyone at the table was wondering what Miss Polly's "short speech" would be.

Miss Polly arose. "It's goodby time, tonight," she began. "Tomorrow the Partridge Family leaves, and they're going to be busy people going on to music and fun and excitement. My nephew says there's lots of practice in store for them before that! They will be giving a concert, as you may know. You, Mr. Harris, and Alison and Courtney will be on your way to California and new plans. Soon Jenny will be off to college and her family back to the workaday world in the city. I, too, shall be leaving. I . . . well, there've been happy times here, and . . . and . . . others." Miss Polly's voice dropped for a moment, but she finished briskly. "Reuben is kindly driving me back to my apartment."

Then she paused, and a smile lighted her face. "I can well remember all I have left to say. Reuben and I have talked it over. We think a new Chestnut Lodge is needed, something spic and span and cheery. The owner of this very hotel thinks so, too. I've agreed to sell the lodge to him, and he will start work right away. The gorge nearby will be deeded to the State as a wilderness preserve."

She paused again. "Now you all have heard of the Polly Kinkaid Scholarship Fund I've been meaning to set up. A tidy sum has come to me from the airlines as a reward for the lost money." She looked down at the table for a moment. "We've talked about just about everything here this evening but the one thing we all have on our minds. I've asked Danny Partridge to speak for me on this."

She sat down and Danny pushed back his chair.

"Miss Polly means Tom Sadd," Danny began. "We can't think of him as Elmer Tell." He swallowed. "Miss Polly was talking to Chris and me about how we'd lost interest in rock hunting. She said that was too bad because that was the one thing real about Tom. He knew a lot about what he was talking about when it came to rocks."

He paused, then went on. "Anyhow, we told her how Tom said rock hunting was a 'big study,' and it gave Miss Polly an idea. So now she has the airlines reward, she's going to have a separate scholarship just for kids who want to study geology—that's the science of rocks. And she's not going to call it the Polly Kinkaid Scholarship Fund. It's just going to be called 'The Big Study Scholarship.' "

As he sat down, there were nods and exclamations of agreement all around the table. Before they died away, Mr. Harris stood up.

"This may not be goodbye time, as Miss Polly said, after all. Reuben Kinkaid suggested that I tell you two pieces of news: Jenny will be definitely hearing from Frameway Films about a part in another movie."

There was applause, and Jenny flushed pink with excitement and pleasure.

"And now for the second announcement," Mr. Harris smiled. "Frameway Films would like The Partridge Family to star in a movie next spring."

There were excited cries from every person at the table. Maribelle Jennings threw her arms around Tracy. "Oh, just think—my best friend a movie star!" she shrieked joyfully.

But Mr. Harris raised his hand. "There's just one thing, though," he said seriously. "We would demand a solemn promise—*six* Partridges must agree to be in *one* movie *together*."

Six Partridges exploded into cheers and laughter. Danny Partridge rocked back and forth in his chair.

"That's about the only way you'll get us, Mr. Harris," he gasped. "*Together!*"

2-73